SHERLOCK HOLMES

The Curse of Pharaoh

Christopher D. Abbott

Other Titles

CONTENTS

Other Titles

SHERLOCK HOLMES

The Curse of Pharaoh

Introduction

On the 16th June 2018, John Turner, a contract builder, was employed to perform renovating work in an unused wing of the lower halls of the British Museum. The decision to remove a wall from a storage room to increase its size had come after years of build-up from accumulated treasures. One of the major tasks undertaken was to improve the lighting facilities within the storage compartments, which would require the removal of the existing steam plumbing in favour of a modern solution.

John Turner and his companions began the task of removing the supporting wall, and when testing holes were drilled though to establish the depth of each cavity, they hit a solid obstacle. As the plans for the lower halls were not accurate, they decided to gently remove the limestone and horsehair plaster to get a better look. Thinking it might have been an iron support, they were surprised to discover a well-preserved Victorian safe. For some reason it had been bricked over after its installation. John Turner instructed his men to stop work and reported it to the senior administrator of the museum.

Brief searches through archive documents gave no

indication as to why the safe had been hidden there. A professor of Victorian history was called to examine the safe. After a lengthy investigation, he ordered it opened. Inside they discovered some ancient Egyptian relics, thought lost, but the most startling thing he discovered was a handwritten manuscript by the famous Doctor John Watson.

No one can answer why Watson's manuscript had been sealed inside. The idea of a safe hidden inside a wall is perhaps a case worthy of Holmes himself. Whatever the reason, a new story in the Holmes canon is reason to cheer. It is, therefore, our privilege to present *Sherlock Holmes: The Curse of Pharaoh*, a brand-new, unpublished case from the world's greatest detective.

Baron Andrew Davies-Gray,
British Museum

Chapter One

'The game is afoot, my boy.'

Readers of *The Times* may recall the chilling events that led to the death of one of the most prominent professors in the field of archaeology in the year 1888. For days on end, London and much of Europe followed the events that sparked a controversy within the great society of the British Museum and questioned the very nature of ancient curses left by long dead civilisation.

What was not known then, and can be revealed now, are the events leading up to the discovery of a carefully planned murder and how my friend, Mr Sherlock Holmes, unmasked a malignant villain while at the same time saving the lives of many people working at the British Museum.

* * *

It had been almost seven years since I'd consented to join with Sherlock Holmes in the rooms of 221b Baker Street. During that time, I'd had the privilege to witness the continued development of his exceptional intellect and deductive skills.

Holmes continued to tally many successfully concluded high-profile cases, ones which, I'm bound to say, had left other official agencies in perplexed ignorance. His professionalism when he reached a conclusion was always a matter of great pride for me. But I suspect it won't surprise my readers to know that paradoxically, he often displayed an indifference to the adulation I heaped upon him. Well, almost. Despite his somewhat laissez-faire attitude, I like to think I know him better than that.

The time we'd spent together was an odd intermix of periods of joy, thrill, and frustration for us both. There came for me a sense of wonder and youthful exuberance when the game was afoot, but for Holmes? His mind remained unemotionally unattached, concentrating only on improving those incredible abilities for his next case. I often thought he decried what I wrote as the thrill of the chase. It was nothing more than a by-product of Holmes's meticulous investigative work. Indeed, I would go so far as to say any stimulation it gave me was utterly lost upon him. I now know that is incorrect. Holmes had become less machine with each new case. The pleasures of hunting and locating criminals, especially where others had been unsuccessful, were *not* lost on him at all. He was simply less inclined to admit it.

A record number of influenza cases kept me busy for several weeks, so I'd not been available to Holmes for a number of his cases. A fact he pointed out as often as he could. His complaints, whilst a little annoying, were not unwarranted. It was one evening in May that Holmes, in an uncustomary display of concern, correctly deduced my fatigue, from the long days of my work, was affecting my health. It was his suggestion that I hand my practice to a neighbour, and take a well-earned break. And so, on that cool night, after an evening meal and brandy, we huddled around the warmth of our fire and reminisced over old cases, Holmes smoking his long-stemmed cherry-wood pipe, and I with a cigar.

Mrs Hudson brought us coffee and for the first time in many days, I relaxed and felt content.

It was later that evening, when I was just slipping into that unconscious contentment further, that the pull-bell rung at our door, waking me. Holmes crossed to the window and looked out. He then turned back to me with a raised eyebrow. I checked the time.

'It's a little late, isn't it?' I said, allowing irritation to slip into my voice. I was just thinking about going to bed.

Holmes straightened the chairs.

'Indeed. However, since it *is* late, we might consider seeing the rather agitated young man before sending him on his way? Unless you'd prefer your bed?'

I made no reply.

'Excellent. I believe that's a footfall on our stair. It might be helpful if you made a note of things, Watson. If only to keep you from falling asleep?'

Again, I said nothing.

Mrs Hudson appeared shortly after with our visitor and Holmes beckoned the man inside, seating him beside the fire. I settled in a chair with my notepad opened. Our guest was a little over thirty years in age. His complexion was lightly bronzed. He was clean-shaven, except for some fashionable sideburns cut long down his checks, and his mousy-brown hair was neatly short. His rather thin eyebrows sat high above his sapphire-blue eyes. They gave him an expression of permanent surprise. The suit he wore was tailored stylishly with pinstripes. Our guest nervously ran a felt-topped silk-lined bowler in his hands as Holmes settled into the chair opposite.

'Mr Holmes,' he said, his voice shaky. 'It is most urgent... No, imperative that I seek your advice. And I pray to God that you can help me; if not, all is lost and I shall be finished.' The blurted cry completed, he sunk his shoulders and slumped back into his chair.

'My dear Mr Johnson...' Holmes paused as our client jumped in shock.

'How in God's name did you know who I am?'

Holmes sighed. 'I did not intend to upset your already agitated state. If you wish to remain incognito then I suggest, for future reference, that you keep your hat brim placed downwards and towards your person, and not towards me where your name is neatly sewed and therefore easily read on the inside rim.'

Our client sat down and nervously smiled. 'I apologise, sir.'

Holmes gave a tight smile, his eyes ablaze with curiosity. 'If you wish to consult me upon whatever made you come out at such a late hour, then furnish me with the facts.'

He nodded. 'I must first ask if you have seen this evening's edition of *The Times*?'

Holmes raised an eyebrow at me, and I got up to check the papers on our table. I shook my head. Holmes opened a box of cigarettes and offered our client one, and he and Holmes shared a match.

'As Watson just confirmed, we have not received the evening edition.'

Our client shrank a little further into the chair. Holmes leant forwards and gave him a gesture of encouragement.

With a haunted expression, Johnson said, 'They say you can read the secrets of your clients, even when they have uttered but a single word.'

'They overestimate my powers,' he answered. 'Beyond the obvious fact that you are well travelled, prefer an open-trap carriage when in London, have not slept for some time, and are a senior clerk at the British Museum, I can deduce nothing.'

Not surprisingly, our client was awestruck at Holmes's casual method of imparting his observations. I had picked up on some of these fairly simple deductions myself. Still, the effect of the nonchalant way in which he made them caused some distress to our client. He shook his head in disbelief.

'I cannot see...'

'Tut, tut, a trifle,' Holmes interrupted impatiently. 'Come, sir, how do I know that you are also a bachelor, and that you have a most slovenly housekeeper?'

These observations surprised me. Our young client looked

between us. I must have been mirroring his tell-tale dumb-founded expression, because Holmes sighed at me.

'You see all, yet you both fail to observe. The dust! The dust!'

At my continued blank expression, Holmes turned to our client.

'Kindly observe the index finger of Mr Johnson's right hand. You will note, on its tip, smudges of that dark-grey dust which accumulates, amongst other things, on the very tops of books. The smudges, though faded, were made no later than this morning. When to this accumulation of dust you add an unbrushed hat, it requires small guile to establish that Mr Johnson has no wife, but an appalling housekeeper.

'When I see a gold-crested ornament hanging from a pocket watch stamped with the crest of the British Museum for long service, and that a typewriter is frequently used, as I observe by not only the indentations of the forefingers and thumbs, but the double-horizontal marks on the wrists – where a person would rest his hands – I can naturally conclude a clerk or similar at that establishment. Long service and quality of clothing suggests a senior rather than junior position.'

'How remarkable!' our young client said.

'Observable,' said Holmes.

'But come, Mr Holmes. You've explained everything but the open trap and the travelling, how could you know my method of transport?'

Holmes was about to answer when he noticed me lean forward. He smiled. 'Watson, I feel, may have the answer to that.'

'The splashes of mud upon your trousers, thrown up by the wheels of the trap?'

'Excellent, Watson. A man who has walked to his destination does not appear with three, four-inch splash marks of fresh clay upon his trousers. It is also visible, in certain lights, where you have brushed similar splashes off previously. You have a bronzed skin you scarcely gained in the climate of this country.'

'First-rate, Mr Holmes. You must have guessed my nervous state as being due to a lack of sleep? Well, you are correct on all accounts.'

'Mr Johnson,' remarked Holmes coolly. 'I never guess. Now explain your situation.'

Our young client visibly relaxed as he told his story.

'Very well, Mr Holmes, before I give you the facts of the case, I would like you to read this article first.' Our client handed Holmes a cut-out copy of the paper. For ease of reading, I have only reproduced the relevant portion of the text:

THEFT AT THE BRITISH MUSEUM!

A valuable golden egg, from an archaeological dig within Egypt's Valley of the Kings, has been stolen from the British Museum under suspicious circumstances. Our reporter has learnt that an examination is being conducted by the famous Scotland Yarder, Inspector Lestrade. There is little information coming from the police, but our reporter has been able to determine that the inspector has begun questioning several employees, who were all working during the time the theft was reported to have taken place. A source close to The Times *suggests the direction their investigation is leading points clearly to an insider.*

The museum has yet to make a comment, but our source has suggested the police are directing their enquires onto a Daniel Johnson, an employee who suspiciously disappeared at some point after he was questioned. Although there is nothing to corroborate it, we believe – and presumably the police do as well – that Johnson must be the insider. With Inspector Lestrade on the case, it can only be a matter of time before Johnson is rightfully in custody.

Holmes gave a series of chuckles as he read through the paragraph, before handing it back to our client.

'*The Times*'s journalistic bias aside, I really cannot explain how you are at liberty at all.'

'You now see how perilous my situation is? I can tell you, Mr Holmes, it was the information I gave during my interview that I believe pushed my name into the forefront of the inspector's list of suspects.' Holmes held up a hand and casually walked over to the window and looked out.

'We haven't much time,' Holmes remarked, as he stepped back from the window and resumed his seat. 'You were followed here.'

With interruption now certain, he said, 'You must detail your story as best you can. When the police arrive, I will try to bargain more time for you. Proceed as succinctly as possible.'

Our client relayed his story and Holmes closed his eyes, relaxing himself into that posture he usually assumed when absorbing information.

'I work, as you correctly surmised, as the supervising clerk to the antiquities department in the British Museum. I look after the administration needs for three separate archaeological professors who work in the field. A week ago, that is to say Tuesday of last, Professor Jeremy Kartz sent me a shipment of artefacts he'd discovered in a tomb in the Valley of the Kings. They made their journey on a cargo vessel to England. Within the trove were treasures dating from the eleventh dynasty. The Egyptian wing is being refurbished to accommodate his discoveries, with a plan to have it opened by the second of July. Mr Holmes, I've not in my lifetime seen such wonders as those I found upon opening the crates. There were jewels, gold of every description, and wonders that...'

'No doubt,' said Holmes with a sigh. 'Please stick to the facts.'

Our client stuttered at the interruption. 'Yes, of course, sorry. In an independent container, locked and padlocked, I found a beautiful golden egg.'

'Independent how?' Holmes made a note on his cuff.

Our client looked puzzled by the question. 'The design of the box was unique and differed from the others. I assumed, because of its size and value, Professor Kartz had organised and packed the egg independent to the other treasures.'

Holmes seemed distracted for a second.

'It is interesting that you should use the word *independent*.

Interesting and suggestive. What then did you do, Mr Johnson?'

'I received specific instructions in two communications. The first instructed me to catalogue the items and inform the various department heads they could begin their work. The second informed me to secure the egg in a separate container and have it ready to be cleaned and valued.'

'Just a moment,' Holmes interrupted. 'Two communiqués? What form did each take?'

'The first came with the bulk of the treasure. There was a full itinerary and instructions.'

'And the second?'

'That came from the telegraph office within the museum.'

'Both were from Kartz?'

'Yes, sir.'

'I see, thank you.' Holmes was thoughtful for a moment. 'This second telegraph. Was it a general message to all the staff?'

'No, it was for my explicit attention.'

'And how did *you* receive it?'

'Like all telegraphs, they first go to the office of Doctor Warmsley. They are secured into individual mailboxes. Doctor Warmsley's secretary handed me mine.'

Holmes nodded with a smile. 'What was the delay in time between the shipment arriving and the second telegraph?'

'The second telegraph came in about three hours after I had signed for the shipment.'

Again, Holmes made notes on his cuff.

'One last question. Did the itinerary list the stolen item?'

'No, it did not. That was only mentioned in the second telegraph.'

Holmes nodded with a satisfied look upon his keen, angular face. 'And that settles matters. Now continue with your very interesting story.'

Our client sat back into his chair and picked up where he had left off.

'Upon receiving the artefacts, I immediately informed the antiquities manager, Doctor Alistair Gough, that I'd entered them into stock. Each is issued a catalogue number and stored in the facility.'

At the pause I looked up to observe, for the briefest of moments, that our client wrung his hands and his face took on a pained expression.

'You can imagine my complete horror, Mr Holmes, when Doctor Warmsley explained that one item in my catalogue was missing. We went to the storeroom, as I was sure there had to be a simple explanation. He'd overlooked it, possibly. Or I'd mistakenly put it into another container.'

Our client looked over at me for a split second, took a breath, then fixed his eyes back on Holmes.

'When I looked in the holding box, it was empty. The golden egg was gone. But I know, *I know*, I put it in there.'

Holmes extinguished his cigarette and replaced it with a clay pipe, which he stuffed and lit.

'Were the police called?'

Johnson nodded and sagged his shoulders. 'Yes, sir. The police arrived with remarkable speed. Inspector Lestrade examined the box and checked the area carefully and diligently.'

'Did he indeed?' Holmes gave a slight cough, but soon waved for our client to continue.

'A door which adjoins a closed wing of the museum was open. That door is always locked. I saw fresh footprints across the dusty floor. The inspector immediately ordered the museum closed. The constables checked each person on exit for the missing item. They found nothing. Inspector Lestrade explained it was likely a member of the public had wandered into the room and found the casket. He believed it was an opportunistic theft.'

Holmes ran the tip of his pipe over his lip.

'But you didn't believe that to be so?'

He shook his head. 'No, Mr Holmes, I did not.'

'Why?'

'I'm no expert in matters of theft, but it seems to me there should be two sets of footprints. One in and one out. There was only the set going out.'

'You impress me, Mr Johnson,' said Holmes, who stood and laid his long arm on the mantel above the fire. 'What else turned you against this theory of the inspector's?'

'It was the simple fact that the casket had been closed up so neatly. Why would a thief close the box at all? Whoever had taken the egg must have known it was there. They *must* have.'

'Ah, I see. Your logic is flawed, I'm afraid,' Holmes said, his eyes finding mine. I knew what that look meant.

Johnson stopped his narrative and looked up at him. 'Oh? Are you sure?'

Holmes flashed me another look. Johnson could not have failed to read the meaning behind it. At length Holmes turned and smiled. 'Surely an experienced thief may have closed the casket intentionally, to ensure its loss was undetected for a longer period?'

'Well… what if it wasn't done by an experienced one?'

'No, no. All the evidence you've laid before me rules that out. We can eliminate chance or random theft. Let us start by inferring one of two possible motives. The first is, the thief knew what to look for.'

'As I have previously said…'

'Indeed. It fits the facts as you've presented them.'

'And the second?'

Holmes leant forward. 'The thief opted to take a smaller item that could, conceivably, be missed for some time. This also supports the facts, yes?'

Johnson nodded.

'Then given the second point, it is possible, however unlikely, that the thief did *not* know of the existence of this egg beforehand?'

'I understand. However, before you rule it out completely, there is something I wish you to consider. The thief had opened four independent locks requiring a different key for each, and a padlock. Once taken, the box was closed and they then secured each lock. Do *you* see? I could understand closing the lid, for who would know that the locks were not closed also?'

Holmes relit his pipe. 'Again, you impress me. Go on.'

'Then there's the lack of footprints coming to the storeroom. It suggested a thief came in from another direction. Lastly, the door to the unused wing can only be unlocked from the inside. That means a thief must have had a key. It is possible to exit the museum from that door in the wing, but only if the door is unlocked. Which under nearly all circumstances it isn't. You see where this is leading?'

'Indeed,' remarked Holmes. He remained thoughtful. During this brief interlude, I took it upon myself to ask an obvious question.

'I take it the room is sound restricted and any noise made would not have reached the upper levels?'

'That's right, Doctor.'

Holmes raised an eyebrow. 'Sound proofing? That again is suggestive.' He turned his attention to the mantel and drummed his finger as he thought.

'How long had the box stood in the storeroom before the theft was discovered?'

Mr Johnson thought for a moment. 'About six hours I would suggest.'

'And in that six hours, in your estimation, how many people would have had access to that room?'

'I would say no more than five, Mr Holmes.'

Holmes nodded in satisfaction. 'Both of you see the point of these questions?'

'Yes,' I answered. 'The theft could have occurred at any point within the six-hour period.'

'Excellent, Watson. No one would know that someone had removed the egg until they opened the box. More evidence I would offer to suggest the thief acted with a detailed knowledge of the operations of the museum.' Holmes then smiled at both of us.

'So, we *are* looking for an inside man?' I asked.

'I think we have established that conclusively. Don't you?' I nodded. 'That would also suggest they *did* know what they were looking for?' I offered.

'It all points that way, I agree.'

'They *had* to know,' our client said, looking down at his hands.

'However,' Holmes said with a smile. 'It is a capital mistake to theorize in absence of the full facts. Let us not be too quick to form opinions. I agree it is a good starting point, but my data is incomplete.'

Holmes took his pipe out of his mouth and tapped it against his chin in thought. It was obvious to me he was pleased with our client, whom he later said had a fresh and open mind.

'Thank you, Mr Johnson. Your observations are accurate and precise. You seem to have done a thorough job. By the process of elimination, we have successfully countered the argument of the police. Although I am loathe to jump to conclusions, the facts do point to a person with existing knowledge of this golden egg.'

Our client flushed red with the praise from the great detective. I admit to a feeling of admiration too. It was rare for Holmes to praise anyone in such a manner.

'That is what I had hoped, and feared, you would say Mr Holmes. For these observations of mine put me in the mess I find myself in. The police became suspicious of me. Since I had a detailed knowledge of the theft, it wasn't long before Inspector Lestrade asked me for *my* movements. When I could not verify them adequately, he asked me to produce my keys. I was astounded to find that they were missing.'

'How were you at liberty to leave? I know Lestrade well. It amazes me he didn't arrest you and half the staff immediately.'

'I think it was in his mind, but as they had searched me and my offices and not found the stolen items, they eventually let me go.'

Holmes nodded. 'Lestrade put an officer on you. And if I am not mistaken, we'll soon have the pleasure of his company.'

It wasn't long before I heard heavy footsteps on our stairs. Holmes opened the door and beckoned in Lestrade before he'd reached the top.

'Mr Holmes,' he said, the exertion of his climb clear from his ruddy complexion. 'Well? Where is he?'

Holmes stretched out an arm and pointed to our client.

'Sitting right here, Lestrade. Where else would you expect him to be? I noticed Watkins lurking across the road.'

Inspector Lestrade smiled as he pulled out a set of cuffs. 'Telling you all his woes, no doubt?'

'Not really. Mr Johnson was explaining the circumstances behind his imminent arrest. I am bound to say, my old friend, there are some questions your theory just can't explain.'

Lestrade turned a shade of red. 'Meaning I have the wrong man?'

'I fear so.'

The inspector paused, collecting his thoughts. At length he said, 'At the moment, Mr Johnson here is the key to my enquiries. Does that satisfy you, Mr Holmes?'

'Somewhat,' Holmes said, with a smile.

'I take it you're finished with him?'

'Not quite. If you wouldn't mind, Lestrade? There are a few questions I would like to ask, before he helps you with your enquiries. I mean, if it's not an imposition?'

'Well,' Lestrade said, looking between us. 'It's a little irregular, but I won't deny you've been helpful to me a few times in the past.' He nodded, and Holmes put a hand on his shoulder.

'But I'll just make myself feel a little better and put these irons on him.'

'Is that necessary?' I asked to our client's dismal groan.

'It's procedure, I'm afraid,' remarked Lestrade with a little wink I didn't care for at all.

Holmes went back to the mantel. 'Very well, Mr Johnson. There are some points I would like to be clear upon. Who knew of the existence of the egg?'

15

'Professor Kartz, myself, Doctor Gough, and Doctor Warmsley.'

'Just these four people? In the entire world?'

Our client shifted in his seat. 'I can't know for certain who at the dig site knew. Some did, obviously. But at the museum, only the three of us, I assure you.'

'Thank you. Who had keys to this unusual casket?'

'Just myself, and Doctor Warmsley. Oh, and Professor Kartz.'

'Why not Doctor Gough?'

'He didn't have any cause to review artefacts in storage, Mr Holmes.'

'So, just the three sets then?'

'That I know of.'

'What would happen if you were to lose a set? How would they be replaced?'

'Oh well, yes, in that instance there is a master set where copies are made,' Mr Johnson added.

'So, at least four sets? Possibly more. Thank you. Now, did you or anyone else observe anything out of place? Anything unusual outside of the theft?'

Mr Johnson thought for a moment. 'I suppose… I mean, it's probably nothing, but there was a spillage of plaster now I come to think about it. On one desk. When I mentioned it, Doctor Warmsley told me he'd been making a cast of an Egyptian mask. We do that from time to time, for the local schools. In all the confusion, we must have knocked it over. I'd put it out of my mind until now.'

'Interesting.'

'But hardly of any relevance,' Lestrade said, rolling his eyes.

Holmes drummed his fingers on the mantel. He had that faraway look in his eyes. After a period of some minutes, our client looked in my direction and frowned. Lestrade checked his pocket watch and gave an audible sigh.

Holmes clapped his hands, which made us all jump. He then rubbed them together. I noticed that sparkle in his eyes which meant he'd discovered something of interest.

'Capital, Mr Johnson, capital. I shall visit the museum tomorrow, with your permission, Inspector?'

Lestrade nodded.

'I can assure you of my fullest attention in this matter.'

Lestrade smiled. 'Our young friend here spins a wonderful story, but story it is. Facts can't be avoided. There had to have been an inside man. And now we discover that there could be any number of keys out there. Keys that Mr Johnson conveniently can't locate.' He opened the door and a constable came in.

'I tell you, Inspector, I do not know what happened to them.'

'Likely story,' Lestrade said, squaring his chin. He turned to the officer at the door. 'Take Mr Johnson to the station, Constable.'

With our client now being marched to the waiting police carriage, Lestrade turned to Holmes, his imperiousness replaced now by a softer expression.

' 'Mr Holmes, I won't deny the evidence against him is circumstantial. But I must start my investigation in my own little way. I think there's something much bigger going on than a few missing trinkets, don't you?'

'My thoughts are leading in that direction,' Holmes said.

Lestrade nodded. 'I'll hold him for twenty-four hours. We'll investigate his story and see if we can't find something to corroborate what he's saying. I know there's an insider. It *could* be him.'

'It *could* be anyone,' I remarked.

'True, but only Professor Kartz, Johnson, Doctor Gough, and Doctor Warmsley knew about that little trinket. And one of them is in Egypt. The other two had alibis. What am I to do, Doctor?'

Holmes put a finger against his lips. 'You must follow your procedures. The law is the law.'

'Exactly.' He turned to leave, then stopped and looked back at Holmes. 'I can't put a finger on it, but I feel like a fish surrounded by sharks on this one.'

Holmes nodded. 'I understand that feeling well.'

Lestrade ran his hat in his hands. 'I'd be obliged if you could lend me some advice, unofficially, you understand?'

'I will update you once I have visited the museum.'

Lestrade put on his hat. 'I'll let Sergeant Wilson know to expect you.'

He tipped his hat to us both and left.

'I've never seen Lestrade so willing to be on our side,' I remarked.

'He's out of his depth, and he knows it.'

'Do you think there's more behind this affair than we're seeing?'

Holmes shrugged. 'Until we have *all* the facts, I don't know. But my instinct says Lestrade is right.'

'That's not something I hear you say often,' I said, chuckling.

Holmes laughed. He put a hand on my shoulder and said, 'The game is afoot, my boy. Are you in for the long haul?'

'You even need to ask?' I said, matching his merriment. Holmes gave my shoulder a squeeze, then disappeared into his bedroom.

Chapter Two

'Bring your trusty revolver, just in case.'

The following morning, I reached the breakfast table to find Holmes eating with gusto. He poured my coffee as I sat. When I thanked him, he returned his attention to the large plate of scrambled eggs and kippers he was devouring. After we had our fill, Holmes replenished our cups with more coffee and broke the silence of our eating by asking me one of the strangest questions he had ever uttered at breakfast.

'Watson,' he said between mouthfuls of coffee. 'What is the greatest number by which three-hundred sixty-five and five-hundred thirty-three can be divided, to leave a remainder of five in each case?'

I looked up, a little taken aback by the question, but as mathematics had always been a strong subject with me, I easily answered it. 'Twenty-four, I believe.'

Holmes gave me an odd frown, and to startle me further, let out a brief laugh and darted across to a blackboard he'd perched against the mantel. I watched with curiosity as he began feverishly writing many pairs of numbers.

'Excellent, Watson, excellent. Twenty-four it is. That

settles the matter.'

I admit to feeling unsure how my answering a simple question had elicited the exultant response, but I said nothing. I watched as Holmes continued to write upon the board.

'It was a rudimentary mistake which led to my vexation over, what turned out be, an elementary conundrum. It was, nevertheless, an interesting and stimulating mathematical puzzle. But I digress. Mycroft employed me to decode a new cipher designed by the Navy. Since you have confirmed my figures, the answer to the problem lies in grouped batches of five… Well, I won't bore you with the details as I'm sure it would agitate Mycroft and the Navy were I to did so. The cipher, as it turned out, comprises of days, a specific historical reference, and hours. A peculiar system they seemed convinced was unbreakable.'

'How long did it take you to beak it?'

'Less than a day, thanks to you.'

I chuckled as Holmes covered the board again and returned to the table.

'I can now add another key to the monograph I'm writing on secret forms of writing. The practical applications should be of some use to the security fraternity. But we can dispense with this, for I see you are unfocused. Your thoughts dwell on our client?'

'Yes. I feel sorry for the poor fellow languishing in Lestrade's dungeon, while we eat our breakfast. I'll be happier once we work on releasing him from his imprisonment.'

Holmes shook his head.

'At present, our young client is far safer in the hands of Lestrade than if he were anywhere else.' Holmes passed me the morning *Times* and pointed to the front-page article.

'Read this.'

THE CURSE OF OSIRIS

A second blow to the British Museum fell today when eminent archaeological professor, Jeremy Kartz, died under tragic and mysterious circumstances. The report, which came in this morning from Egypt, indicated Kartz died suddenly in an antiquities presentation of which he was guest of honour. Egyptian sources close to the Antiquities Service are believed to be playing down rumours of an ancient Pharaoh's curse. Local people are vocal about a papyrus text Kartz apparently uncovered at the dig site. The alleged 2000-year-old text warns of a violent death to anyone who disturbs the resting Pharaoh's tomb.

"Professor Jeremy Kartz died from trauma to his heart and certainly not by any ancient curse," said eminent French Egyptologist Anton Bouchard, head of the Egyptian Antiquities Service. "All sane people should dismiss such inventions with contempt."

The British Museum released a statement saying: "We do not recognise superstitions or curses." They go on to say: "The British Museum's position is clear. We believe in scientific explanations for Professor Kartz's cause of death, which is on record as myocardial infarction." When asked about the health of the professor, a spokesman added: "We have no comment regarding Professor Kartz's health. Archaeological excavation is not easy work. There are many stresses and pressures that come as a result of it. We understand the need for public scrutiny, but ask that foremost consideration be given to Professor Kartz's family at this time. The British Museum will make no further comments on Professor Kartz's death."

'This is foreboding news, Holmes. I've studied the physiology of curses, and in my experience they're not all as erroneous as they seem, and certainly not all supernatural. Do you know that a virulent disease can lay dormant on decaying flesh, or in the air, and be picked up by unsuspecting archaeologists that are exposed to them? Perhaps this death is nothing more than that.'

Holmes seemed lost in thought. When he spoke, his voice was uncharacteristically soft. It transfixed me totally.

'And it came to pass, that at midnight the Lord smote all the firstborn in the land of Egypt, from the firstborn of the Pharaoh that sat on the throne unto the firstborn of the captive in the dungeon; and all the firstborn of cattle. Pharaoh, his servants, and all the Egyptians rose in the night, and there was a great cry in Egypt; for there was not a house where there was not one death.'

Holmes's eyes were half-closed as he turned to me. Those softly spoken words sent a chill up my spine, and he let out a little grunt of satisfaction at my expression.

'My words moved you?'

'They did,' said I. The thoughts of curses and the dead plagued my thoughts for a while longer. Holmes refilled his morning pipe.

'The mind is very susceptible to suggestion, Watson. You read of the curse of Osiris, I paraphrase from the bible, and there you have it. One psychologically embedded belief of curses. That is how the media use it, and why the Church manages as well as it does.'

'What about the possibility of Kartz being infected by some ancient illness?' I asked to Holmes's shake of head.

'I am surprised at you, Watson. Egyptian curses are primarily a cultural, not exclusively scientific, phenomenon. I think we can rule out such matters without *any* further discussion. Our consideration must be to determining the means of death. Did Kartz die of natural causes or by some pre-existing health condition? Or was he murdered? That his death occurred so swiftly after a major theft is suggestive. I wouldn't be surprised if there are more to add to it soon enough.'

I nodded at his comments. It seemed plausible the theft and subsequent death was connected. I didn't relish the idea of more deaths, though.

Holmes pulled his pipe from his mouth and looked over some documents he had on the table. He slurped at his coffee as he organised his thoughts.

'What do you have there?' I asked.

'These?' he said, handing me the papers. 'I requested all the available information regarding the excavation of Kartz's tomb. I thought they might be of practical importance. Why don't you read through them while I'm out?'

'You're going to the museum? Alone?'

'No, no. Not without you. I need some information first. I'll meet you back here at noon.'

Holmes finished his coffee and moved towards his bedroom. 'You'll be ready for an adventure by the time I return?'

I smiled. 'Of course.'

'Excellent. Bring your trusty revolver, just in case.'

I nodded, and with that he entered his room and closed the door.

Whilst Holmes was out, I studied the documents he'd left me. They were full of fascinating information regarding the late Professor Kartz's discoveries at the ancient Egyptian tomb. Kartz originally believed he'd discovered the tomb of a mystery Pharaoh, but this proved not to be the case.

In the weeks that led to the breakthrough, Kartz and his team were excavating in a small area to the north of the Valley of the Kings, just across the Nile River from the ancient capital of Thebes. Kartz was busy organising a team of workers to remove the debris strewn around the tomb of Amenophis III, discovered by members of Napoleon's Egyptian expedition. It was whilst clearing this area that workers unexpectedly discovered a deep, in-filled trench cut into the hillside. Kartz assumed they'd uncovered a ceremonial gully which originally formed part of Amenophis's tomb. But, when pieces of broken pottery were unearthed, the professor was convinced they'd discovered another tomb. There was disagreement in the direction to pursue, because the season was coming to an end. However, consensus was reached and many days of clearing continued, which rewarded them with a partially revealed flight of carved stairs. This then prompted furious sessions of everlasting all-round digging, until the top of the stairwell was exposed. Kartz's insistence had paid off. For an entire week his men worked hard to clear the rubble and finally, after some thirty-six steps were uncovered, Kartz stood alongside an intact limestone wall, sealing the entrance to his newly discovered tomb.

The reports, though not completed, listed some of the findings. In his own words, he described what he'd discovered. "At first I could see nothing," he wrote, "the hot air escaping from the chamber caused candle flames to flicker. As my eyes grew accustomed to the dim light, details of the room within emerged." He went on to further say, "Excitement gripped us hitherto, and had given us no pause for thought. It was only now I realised just how difficult a task lay before us. With these conflicting thoughts and feelings, I set upon that task with professionalism. Yet in the pit of my mind, I considered the serious implications and perils aligned with maintaining security over such a wondrous find."

Reading through the material and looking at the photographs from the dig gave me a genuine appreciation for the work archaeologists performed. To be able to painstakingly coax history from the sand, and piece those tiny unrecognisable fragments into relics we can identify, is absolutely amazing.

* * *

At exactly noon the door to our sitting room opened and Holmes entered with a flushed face and eager expression.

'How was your morning?' I asked, as he stuffed his clay pipe with tobacco from the Persian slipper.

'Excellent; I must say there's nothing like a stroll to heighten one's appreciation for a meal.'

Holmes's mood was infectious and I detailed the information from the tomb's account. He listened eagerly, occasionally nodding when I said something which he considered of interest.

'You've yet to tell me,' said I, 'where you have been this morning.'

'To the library, Watson, to Egypt! I gathered the most fascinating information regarding ancient Egyptian culture. It is a singular and most dynamic race of people that build pyramids of sand and stone the base of which can cover thirteen acres, an area so vast that it may accommodate the cathedrals of Florence, St Paul's, Westminster Abbey, and St Peter's in Rome, and still have room to spare. If it were not for my current profession, Watson, it is not impossible that I would have taken up the challenge of solving the mystery of how people, only equipped with simple rudimentary tools, could haul and cut thousands of tons of rock and build such a thing. The task should have taken generations to complete, yet surprisingly they managed it in around twenty years.'

The entire time Holmes spoke, he gesticulated with his pipe. There was a delighted, childlike expression upon his angular face.

'You make it sound as though you've only just discovered that pyramids exist!' I said with a laugh.

Holmes shrugged. 'You sound surprised. Until today, I knew practically nothing except that there *were* pyramids. As you well know, I never clutter my brain with useless information. And long-dead civilisations fall well within that rule. My wants for knowledge exist within the present. Perhaps I should have stopped once I had learnt all I needed, but curiosity can be an infectious thing. My research therefore continued. It might surprise you to learn I now have a good understanding of the principles of ancient Egyptian hieroglyphics and can distinguish from various styles, thanks largely to the excellent work of the French scholar, Jean-François Champollion.'

'I am very happy to hear you've increased your knowledge of things outside of crime.'

Holmes puffed on his pipe for a while. He allowed an amused look to form, as his eyes found mine.

'The knowledge will come in use, I feel certain.'

'From an academic standpoint?'

Holmes shook his head. 'For the case.'

I sighed. 'And when this case is complete?'

He shrugged. 'I shall do my best to forget it.'

Why was I not surprised?

'But come,' Holmes said, tapping out his pipe into the fire. 'We must eat. I suggest we pay a visit to our good friend, Rossini, and then make our way to the museum.'

Chapter Three

'Do you imagine I had not already thought of that?'

Our lunch was brief and Holmes spoke little concerning the case. After coffee and a cigar, we departed in a cab for the British Museum. There Sergeant Wilson introduced us to Mr Adrian Gyde, who escorted us to the storage room that was sealed off at the request of the police.

It was large by storage-room standards. Within, lined along the walls, I noticed several ornate trunks of different sizes and types neatly stacked on wall-mounted racks. Each were sequentially numbered. A set of well-used wooden workbenches adorned the south wall, with tools and plaster casts strewn over them in an untidy, haphazard fashion. The door to an adjoining wing was inset on the west wall. The fixtures and fittings started at this door and continued around to the one we'd entered. Mr Gyde explained that since the refurbishment had begun, they were housing a larger than usual number of artefacts in storage.

Holmes took an immediate interest in this door, making detailed searches of the lock, handle, and surrounding floor. I don't suppose anyone had made such a comprehensive examination of a door before, and once his conclusions were formed, seemingly satisfied, he traced the clear footsteps backwards to a wall-mounted rack.

As was his way, he conducted this examination in complete silence. I stood away and watched as Holmes pulled out his small white envelopes and a set of tweezers from a leather toolkit. Each time he stopped at something that caught his eye, he filled the contents of an envelope and hand it to me. After some twenty minutes had passed, Holmes turned his attention to a strongbox on the floor. I noticed earlier that it was opened, and empty. It must surely have been the box containing the golden egg.

Holmes began a visual study of each lock with his glass, then turned to the inside of the container. Nothing was left un-eyed. He painstakingly examined every facet. Once he'd sucked in all the data, he moved to the work benches on the south wall. There, he paid particular attention to the plaster casts, taking samples of both the plaster and wood shavings he found there.

Something on the table seemed to make him hesitate. For the first time, I noticed his hand shook as he ran it above the tools. I curbed the urge to ask questions, as I knew Holmes would not have answered any at that point. It lasted for a moment only, and he continued his investigation by dropping to the flooring. He made a slow route along its dusty surface, his glass attached permanently to his eye, stopping only to fill an envelope with another sample. This detailed investigation continued for another ten minutes, and I couldn't help wondering what Holmes was thinking. Had he already formulated a theory? Had he discovered the perpetrator of the crime?

Holmes stood and held a finger to his closed mouth in deep thought, turning his head from side to side. His eyes found the door, the table, and then the casket. Finally, he walked back to the east door and paced out the dimensions of the room.

'Well,' he said, with a quick shake of his head. 'I'm of a

mind to say that this is a singular room indeed.'

Holmes handed me yet another envelope and brushed the dust from his frock coat.

'Have you discovered anything that might help vindicate our client?' I asked.

Holmes frowned in that way, suggesting he was unhappy.

'It is odd,' he said, to nobody in particular, then turned to me and smiled. 'This room has so many clues as to the identity of our criminal friend, that I can't imagine why Lestrade would have bothered arresting our client at all. It's all wrong. All of it.' He waved a hand around the room, then stared at the floor.

'I can see nothing at all. Everything is as Mr Johnson suggested. The casket is open. The door to the closed wing is open. There are footprints leading out, but not leading in. Tell me what you've seen that I have not?' Holmes always saw more than me. That was a fact. But sometimes, it was necessary to provoke him into revealing information, even if it was at the expense of my obvious stupidity. If I've heard "you see all, yet fail to observe" once, I've heard it a thousand times. Holmes, however, did not point that out to me, which was a surprise.

'First of all, the man is a hair tailer than our client. He is almost certainly Egyptian, or at very least from the Mediterranean. You see here that the right shoe impression is less distinct? It indicates a lameness in that leg. His suit is made from cream linen, the quality of which one might expect from the area of the world he comes from. He had a master key, commonly referred to as a skeleton key. For there are no impressions on the locks that suggest even the most skilled of lock pickers. Our thief smokes Calistow cigarettes, which are peculiar to Egypt and sold almost exclusively there. However, I'm aware of at least one tobacconist in London who imports them, so that doesn't help us much.'

Holmes put his glass back into his pocket and pulled two cigarettes from a silver case, lighting them both, and handing one to me.

'Our thief entered the room and went to that bench first. I found minute traces of a particular type of sand, which is common enough in Egypt, but not, I fancy, in the suburbs of London.'

'Could it have been builder's sand?'

Holmes smiled. 'I thought so too, but once I had enough inside one of my envelopes, I could see through the lens that it was unrefined and course. It has a peculiar odour indicative to the Mediterranean, but as many of these caskets have recently arrived from there, that doesn't aid us either.'

'True,' I said. 'With so much of it lying around, it's probable it came inside the shipment.'

'Precisely,' he remarked, then pointed to the bench. 'The thief smoked a cigarette, stubbing it out here, before opening the west door with a key. Which was a curious thing to do.'

Holmes smoked silently for a time.

'Why do you consider this curious?' I looked around at the door and then at Holmes, who inclined his head.

'You must admit, it's a brazen thing to stand and smoke *before* committing your crime?'

'Meaning he knew time was on his side?'

Holmes smiled at me. 'As if there was no fear of interruption.'

'And the door?'

'My instincts tell me we are dealing with a professional. Why would he need to open that door before setting his mind to the task at hand?'

'To secure his means of a quick escape, surely?'

Holmes touched my shoulder. 'And yet he had time to smoke? The need to establish a quick escape conflicts with this action.'

I nodded. 'It is perplexing.'

'Now we come to the item itself. It is clear that its value is of no concern.'

At this, I frowned. 'You can't know that for certain.'

'I think we can. Look around you, Watson. There are many obvious items of value. Yet the thief chose this specific trinket. Why? He could simply have taken something of equal if not more value from those shelves nearest the door. There are deeper waters here. It's indicating… No. I must not make judgements ahead of the data.'

Holmes's observations were not lost upon me, for I could see the value of his argument. The thief had to have known the golden egg was there, and he knew where to look for it too.

'You think they were trying to frame our client, don't you?'

Holmes flashed me a rare grin. 'That is one of the theories I have. But why? This I cannot adequately answer. But let that be a topic for another time, for we are ahead of ourselves.'

Holmes continued to vocalise his observations.

'Once our intrepid thief had secured his means of escape, he then opened the casket and removed its contents. I found further evidence of his nationality, by traces of dark hair left behind. They had a wax cream still applied, typically used by gentlemen of the Mediterranean, for the waxing balm is a lime and olive derivative, often used as a sun-blocking agent. Our thief locked the container, then exited via the west door disappearing into the crowds of visitors in the vestibule. A remarkably intelligent, carelessly, idiotic man. You see my dilemma?'

'It's an oxymoron.'

'Exactly. Meaning he can't be both. The evidence he left behind should have been obvious, even to our police friends.'

Holmes had a faraway look that I often attributed to him forming theories. I voiced my concern.

'You seem distracted. Can I be of any help at all?'

Holmes broke from his revere and smiled.

'You're always of virtuoso help to me, Watson. You are my motivation, my romantic personification. I'm bound to say that I'm very unhappy with this room. Something about the neatness with which all the clues flow bothers me. There are no less than seventeen different indications here, hardly in character with the profile of a professional thief, wouldn't you say? Crime, like life itself, is built upon a complicated balance of probability and chance. In this case, Watson, all threads lead us to one outcome, whereas there should be many. I believe our thief travelled a similar path to the golden egg from Egypt, to this museum. Both the egg and the thief ended up here, possibly at the same time, and left together, probably re-bound for Egypt.'

Holmes finished his cigarette and stubbed it out.

'How did our thief get to this storage room unseen? But more important than that. Amongst the rabbit warrens of rooms in the under-halls, how did he know where to look?'

'Perhaps he was disguised somehow?' I suggested.

'It's possible, I won't discount it. Let us start with the hypothesis this thief moved through the museum without fear of being caught.'

'Meaning he was known to the staff?'

Holmes nodded. 'Another point in Lestrade's favour.'

'Agreed,' I said. 'Surely that makes it easier for us? We need only discover who entered the room prior to the theft. Employees are required to sign out their keys, aren't they?'

Holmes gave a dismal groan. 'Do you imagine I had not already thought of that?'

'It was just a suggestion.'

'Did I not tell you he had a skeleton key?'

'Yes, but…'

'So then might it be conceivable he owned it, and therefore did not sign it out?'

'True,' I said.

'Also, since our client lost his keys, might I suggest we move on from that line of inquiry?'

'I think we should at least check,' I persisted.

Holmes grunted. 'Well, Watson. If you believe it useful to do so, I will not stop you. Now come. We must question the staff.'

Holmes and I left the storage room and ascended to the upper hall. Our first destination was the office of Doctor Gough, the antiquities manager.

The office was sparsely decorated with a few personal effects. An oak bookcase filled with red and black bound books ran along the wall, and a matching desk covered in papers was all that occupied the room. That, and Doctor Gough, who was a short, unassuming fellow with a ruddy complexion, heavy moustache, and neat beard. He welcomed us curtly and indicated we should sit. Holmes, as always, preferred to stand and waited until Doctor Gough had resumed his seat before speaking.

'You are the antiquities manager, are you not?'

The doctor raised his bushy eyebrows at Holmes. 'I am, sir.'

Holmes nodded and he continued his questioning. 'Did you see the missing golden egg, catalogue number four-three-nine, prior to its theft?'

Doctor Gough shook his head. 'No. I don't normally view these artefacts at all, unless some business of mine required me to see them. Which isn't often, Mr Holmes.'

Holmes inclined his head slightly. 'I understand that the egg was catalogued and stored in the chamber directly below this office. In your opinion, how possible would it be for an unknown person to enter these offices and descend to the chamber below and be unnoticed?'

Doctor Gough leaned forward. 'It would be impossible.'

Holmes nodded. 'As I suspected, thank you. Tell me, what is your opinion of Mr Johnson?'

'He is a good sort, careful, and tidy in his habits. A little overprotective of his charge, but other than that a competent clerk and a highly rewarded one.'

Holmes seemed happy with the assessment and turned to leave. Then a thought occurred and he looked back. 'Would it be possible for a man to enter these offices at night?'

Doctor Gough shook his head. 'I see where this is leading, Mr Holmes. That would also be impossible. There are three night watchmen. Two of which sit directly outside the doors of these offices. It would not be possible for any person, whether known or otherwise, to enter without being seen. Those who work outside of their allotted time must report those intentions to their managers, who will subsequently inform the watchmen.'

'Thank you, Doctor Gough. Your information was most helpful.'

Holmes left the room. After shaking Doctor Gough's hand, I followed him out.

Our second interview was with Doctor Warmsley. He was a very nervous man with bitten, ragged nails, a wiry frame, and light-brown mousy hair. He welcomed us into his office, which was cluttered with paperwork and books, haphazardly spread across the many workbenches and cabinets. Holmes smiled at the doctor and he returned it, a little easier in mind, I thought.

'Sorry for the untidiness with which my room appears. I do have my methods you understand, disarray it may be, but I know where everything is.'

Holmes pulled a seat from the table. 'You'll hear no argument from me. Watson here will tell you I feel quite at home in this type of environment.'

Warmsley was now very much at ease. He offered us some tea that had not long been made, and we accepted gratefully.

'It is a pleasure to meet you, Doctor,' Holmes said. 'That last production of *The Fall of Summer* was a masterpiece, although the final conclusions of the inspector were, shall we say, somewhat vague?'

'Ah,' Warmsley said, a confused look passing over his face. 'You must have me confused with someone else. I know nothing about *The Fall of Summer.*'

'Dear me,' said Holmes at length. 'I am a fool, I could have sworn I saw you in that production, no?'

'Alas...'

'Well, to save myself any further embarrassment, let us move to a topic that you will be aware of. The nature of our visit? Ah, I see that it is so. Had you seen the golden egg prior to its theft of yesterday?'

Warmsley shook his head. 'I had seen the telegram that Kartz, God rest his soul, sent Johnson. It detailed his instructions, but when I went to examine the object, it had already gone.'

Holmes was thoughtful for a second. 'Do you still have the telegram, Doctor?'

Warmsley nodded. He lifted a pile of papers and handed it to him.

'I suspected you'd want to see it, Mr Holmes. I *can* tell you Kartz did not send it. I'm quite certain of that.'

This revelation caused Holmes to grab the telegram from the eager-faced Warmsley and study it carefully. Holmes however seemed disappointed and then folded the paper up and placed it into his pocket.

'How so?' asked Holmes.

'Why? Because he's was a terrible speller, and the telegram is spelt correctly.'

Holmes shook his head in some disbelief. 'The telegram was written by the telegraph operator, they usually are. Kartz would have dictated it.'

Warmsley seemed disappointed by this revelation. 'Oh blast! I was certain I'd cracked it.'

Holmes thanked him for his diligence. 'I was unaware that Kartz was poor at spelling, these are details I like, so I am indebted to you for pointing it out. What can you tell me about Mr Johnson?'

At the mention of our client's name, Warmsley's face furrowed. 'I don't care for the man, Mr Holmes, not one jot. He strikes me as an opportunist. A man of letters he may be, yet works as a clerk when his knowledge of Egyptology surpasses many professors he works under. I was always suspicious of that man.'

Holmes was most attentive throughout the conversation, making small notes on his pad as the conversation continued.

'I was with Kartz and Johnson, one morning, when Kartz was examining a set of hieroglyphics from a dig site just north of Luxor. Kartz made an observation regarding the wording, and Johnson corrected him. I remember he was quite put out by it. Well, he would, wouldn't he? But he conceded Johnson had identified the correct translation. It occurred to me that Johnson knew more than he let on. This was especially clear when he contrived an excuse to cover his slipup. He told the professor he'd recently studied the text. Clever boy, I'll grant you. Johnson suggested he'd only had the knowledge to spot that type of error, because he'd studied Kartz's published works. And Kartz, being sensitive to flattery, accepted this explanation. And there was never a mention of the subject again. But I was positive Johnson was up to something. It's no surprise to hear he's been arrested. It had to happen eventually.'

Holmes's interest was piqued. He seemed lost in thought for a second or two.

'Why did you say he was a man of letters?'

Warmsley shrugged. 'Just an observation. He slipped up frequently. His grammar is almost perfect, his written word unquestionable, and his knowledge of Egyptian history is far greater than he lets on. He wrote a paper on a Pharaoh for Kartz that he said took him several months to complete with much research and sleepless nights. Utter nonsense. Gough told me he wrote it all from memory, and in the space of a few days.'

I admit this revelation left me with more questions unanswered than before. Why would Johnson take up a post beneath his abilities? And why make a pretence at all regarding his knowledge? Holmes however seemed satisfied with the interview and concluded it by saying so. He paused, hit his head with his hand, and rolled his eyes. I frowned. It was an uncharacteristic display.

'My, my,' he said. 'I shall forget my head one of these days. Where might I find the watchman who was on duty the day of the theft?'

'He has the day off, Mr Holmes. There was a family death three days previous and he attends the funeral today. I gave the police his particulars.'

Holmes nodded once. 'Thank you for your time, Doctor. You have given me invaluable information. Especially regarding Mr Johnson.'

'Yes,' he looked regretful. 'My information must have been

difficult to hear, considering you are acting on his behalf. It must surely seem impossible now to save him?'

Holmes said, 'On the contrary. Your information was the last piece of evidence I needed. It will enable me to secure his release from incarceration.'

Warmsley's eyes went wide. 'You're telling me he had nothing to do with it?'

Holmes smiled. 'Come, Watson.'

Holmes was in an energetic mood when we left the offices of the museum. The two interviews seemed to have given him fresh angles, and he proposed we travel at once to see Lestrade.

Our journey to Scotland Yard was uneventful and Holmes said little, preferring instead to smoke and watch London pass us by. Holmes seemed distracted. As was the case when there was silence between us, I began pondering on what thoughts were passing through his great brain. As our journey unfolded, I thought upon the various elements we'd discovered so far. Holmes had concluded Mr Johnson was not responsible for the theft. And our client's observations and deductions were accurate. It was obvious from the clues the thief was from the Mediterranean, which clearly exonerated our client. However, I still had the sense that Holmes was unhappy, although with what I was sure I had no idea.

The carriage pulled up outside the main gates of Scotland Yard and we departed. Holmes pressed the bell to gain attention. Our wait was not a long one, as an officer who recognised Holmes immediately smiled and gestured that he should come through.

Lestrade sat perched in his chair, tapping away at a large typewriter. Both Holmes and I shared a quick look of amusement, as we watched the eminent Lestrade of Scotland Yard cursing at the "wretched machine". Holmes coughed to gain Lestrade's attention, and he looked up over a pair of spectacles.

'I didn't know you used those,' said Holmes with amusement, pointing to the glasses that Lestrade was quickly removing.

'Well, there are things that I *try* keeping to myself, Mr Holmes,' he said. 'What brings you two here then, as if I couldn't guess?'

Holmes sat down in the chair opposite him and placed his hands upon the table.

'Lestrade, I want you to release my client.'

Lestrade gave a long sigh and nodded.

Holmes raised an eyebrow. 'No argument? Are you feeling unwell?'

The inspector laughed. 'In my long experience, Mr Holmes, I know that an argument with you is like teaching a woman the value of money: pointless.'

I knew many independently wealthy women who would disagree in the strongest terms with what Lestrade had said, but kept it to myself.

Lestrade sat back in his chair. 'Give me all the details then. I assume that you're here to disprove my theory completely.'

Holmes waved a hand in the air. 'Not entirely.'

Lestrade sat bolt upright, a look of mock surprise crossing his superior face. 'You mean you haven't discovered the identity of the thief? Well, Mr Holmes. Perhaps it is *I* that should ask you if *you're* feeling well?'

Lestrade sat back in his chair with a chuckle.

'The thief is around five feet, eight inches in height, has a white-cream suit common to men from the Mediterranean. Probably dark skinned. Wears olive-lime extract upon his hair. Smokes Egyptian-branded Calistow cigarettes and knew exactly what he was looking for.'

Lestrade gave a resigned gesture. 'I see.' He paused, then said, 'And where do I look for this mysterious Mediterranean gentleman?'

'Calistow cigarettes are sold, as far as I know, only in Mayfield's on the west bank.'

'I know of it. I'll start my enquires there.'

Holmes drummed his fingers on the table. 'There's something else, Lestrade. I'm not convinced we are dealing with one man, there must be others involved.'

Lestrade nodded. 'Somebody who let the fellow in through the busy offices, gave him a duplicate key and detailed instructions of where to go and how to escape, perhaps?'

Holmes nodded. Despite their adversarial attitude to each other, it was clear there was a friendship between them.

Holmes rubbed his chin. 'We must be dealing with an inside man.'

'But apparently not your client,' Lestrade said. 'Despite the fact that he fits the description.'

'As do three others,' Holmes countered.

'Perhaps we should question him further?' I said.

Holmes looked between us, then shrugged.

'Mr Holmes thinks he's innocent. I say, there's still the possibility he may be complicit.'

Holmes sighed. 'I do not ignore the obvious fact that we are dealing with an inside man.'

'A compromise, then. We don't question Johnson, but let him go. I'll stick a man on him. If he's involved, then let him lead us to the thief. I'll have a man at Mayfield's. We'll start looking out for this mystery Mediterranean as well.'

Holmes nodded, slowly. 'But be wary. If we reveal our hand too soon, the rats will bolt and we'll have nothing.'

Lestrade stood and we both followed.

'Well, gentlemen. I'll release Johnson and post a man at watch. Perhaps you'd like to brief the men on what they should look out for at Mayfield's?'

'Wise. Once they are out, we'll let your men work their own methods.'

'And what if Mr Johnson is innocent?' I asked.

Lestrade shrugged. 'He'll be none the wiser, Doctor. And we'll then need to start other enquiries. Good or bad, we'll get something from him.'

Holmes and I entered a cab and made our way to Baker Street.

'What is the next move?' I asked.

'I need to think on things. There's something underlining this entire affair I can't quite see.' He said nothing more until we reached our doors.

Chapter Four

'There's money in this case, Watson, if there's nothing else.'

The bitter day of May had finally taken its toll on me, as we walked along the cleaned pathways that lead back to the warmth of 221b Baker Street. Time was moving on and I was happy our journey was almost over. That thick characteristic London smog, which had been more plentiful since the erection of a second factory in the vicinity, had made visibility difficult. Thankfully, the gasman had lit the lamps along our walk. I pondered on whether any other country's roads looked more foreboding than a London street did, when the swirl of smog got caught under the hazy glare of these yellow-flamed lamps.

When we entered Baker Street, Holmes and I removed our overcoats. Holmes surprised me by pointing at a large wet footprint on our mat.

'A visitor?' I enquired.

'Surely a large one, given the size of that foot.'

We both discarded our hats as Mrs Hudson greeted us and handed Holmes a card.

'The gentleman has been here for thirty minutes, Mr

Holmes. I made up your fire and a pot of fresh tea for him.' Holmes took the card and smiled. 'Thank you, Mrs Hudson. Could I trouble you for a fresh pot?'

She nodded and shuffled off. Holmes handed me the card.

'Edward Trellorney Stanhope Smith, sixth Earl of Braxton,' I read.

'There's money in this case, Watson, if there's nothing else. Come, let us see what troubles so large a man on so cold a day.'

Holmes shot up the stairs and I followed. When we entered our rooms, we found the heavily framed, six-foot-tall lord standing near our fire.

'Mr Sherlock Holmes?' he enquired as we entered the sitting room.

'I am he,' replied Holmes, closing on the huge form of the lord and reaching for his pipe on the mantel.

'Forgive me, sir, but I have smoked several cigars in my wait. The air is thick, but I feared that to open the window might make a poor effort of this lovely fire that your housekeeper so willing made me upon my arrival.' Never had I heard such a softly spoken man in all my cases with Holmes. Lord Braxton's voice gave us both causes for recoil, of which Holmes quickly recovered.

'How may I be of service, Lord Braxton?' Holmes lit his clay pipe and puffed feverously on it.

'I came to consult you on a private matter,' Lord Braxton said. 'One you may already be investigating. I refer to the death of Professor Jeremy Kartz, and the loss of many artefacts that possibly contributed to it.'

Holmes gestured for Lord Braxton to sit, which he did, and Mrs Hudson arrived with a fresh pot of tea.

'My lord, the police have begun an investigation into reports of stolen artefacts at the British Museum. I have been retained independently in the matter, the priorities of which centre entirely on my client. What reasons do you have for believing Professor Kartz's death and these thefts are linked?'

I watched the great man wrestle with some heavy

42

questions, and finally he stood and paced the floor.

'Professor Kartz was a sturdy man with years of experience behind him. I can tell you he had no kind of heart condition. It's all press speculation, in my opinion. As far as I know, he had nothing that would attribute to his horrendous death.'

'People may have underlying health issues that we don't see during routine medical checks,' I pointed out.

He nodded. 'I don't discredit it, Doctor. Of course, you're right. But the fact is, I'm very close friends with his physician, and he swears on his children's lives that Kartz did not have a heart condition.'

'I see,' Holmes was thoughtful for a moment. 'And because of this affirmation only, you've come to a conclusion that both events must be connected?'

'You doubt it?'

'I have no data,' Holmes remarked. 'What do you suggest I conclude from this connection?'

'That Kartz was murdered, sir. Unless you wish to believe he died of some damnable curse?'

Holmes chuckled and pointed to the seat again. 'Sit, Lord Braxton. I believe many of your observations are correct. Professor Kartz was almost certainly murdered. I have given little thought to a motive, but greed would seem to be an obvious choice. However, in order for me to investigate, it would require a visit to Egypt. Now my client, who is at this moment being released from his incarceration, hired me to locate a missing golden egg, which I have yet to do.'

'But surely you can see that this egg artefact is inconsequential. Isn't it possible that once you find the killer, you might also find the egg?' interrupted Lord Braxton.

Holmes smiled. 'That may be so, but I do not believe we have exhausted all our options in England.'

Clouds of smoke billowed around Holmes, as he drew on his pipe in thought. Then his eyes found Braxton, and he gave a slow smile.

'There is another reason you're here, is that not so?' asked Holmes.

The earl looked a little white in the face and sombrely nodded. 'I see it is pointless to hold back any details from you.'

'Quite so!' Holmes exclaimed.

'As you know, the tomb excavation particularly interests the world of archaeology. I am told there is not a professor in Europe who is not excited by the find. Only a select few people know that I—'

'That you are the sole provider of financial support for the dig?' interrupted Holmes to a momentary look of surprise from his lordship.

'Yes. That's it, exactly,' he remarked. 'I must congratulate you on your thorough search, Mr Holmes, although I am sure that you could not have found that information out at the museum. I would be interested to know where you did.'

Holmes smiled. 'You forget, my lord. I am a detective,' Holmes said, rather too quickly for my liking. 'Now, pray continue.'

Lord Braxton extinguished his cigar and took some tea.

'I have always been interested in archaeology. As a boy it was my dream to discover hidden treasure, but like most boyhood dreams, they disappear when adulthood – and the responsibilities that one's station dictates – arrives. When Professor Kartz asked me for financial support I was, truthfully, wary. He had an excellent reputation, so after some thought, I considered his proposal. Let me tell you, I have never regretted that decision. Not once. Archaeology furnishes a scholarly pursuit with all the excitement of a gold prospector's life. His first message to me was amazing. "We've made a wonderful discovery in the Valley. A magnificent tomb, seals intact. Details to follow."

'When Professor Kartz sent me that news, I was overjoyed. My poor wife was almost driven mad by my excitement of it. The wire explained the finds extended from the thirteenth dynasty to the Ptolemaic period. It was a rich find. It included sarcophagi, furniture, musical instruments, toys, and an inlaid board of games. His wire detailed many hieratic and demotic texts of great historical interest. Jeremy Kartz was not only a talented archaeologist, but a kindred spirit. I was keen he should continue digging, but my accountant brought the not-inconsiderable expense of such work home to me. Kartz came up with the business-like suggestion that expenses of the work might be defrayed by selling some antiquities to collectors, at a handsome profit.'

Holmes tapped out his pipe and Lord Braxton shook his head sadly.

'Everything was going well, until I received the terrible of news of Jeremy's death. You can imagine how horrified I was, and not the least a little suspicious. Then I read the news about Johnson, which shocked me further. I am assuming he is your client?'

'I see no reason to deny it.'

'He strikes me as a dependable fellow. I am pleased you've secured his release from the police. To lose one man in the field is bad enough, but to lose two connected to the same event would be catastrophic. The harm to the archaeology fraternity could not be exaggerated.'

The fire crackled and Holmes looked towards it momentarily, sighed, then finished his tea. Braxton continued unaware of Holmes's apparent distraction.

'I considered for some time what steps were necessary to ensure that this excavation continued and the museum did not lose out. Your name was recommended to me, so I thought to drop the entire thing in front of you, with the aim to persuade you to go to Egypt on my behalf.'

Holmes smoked his pipe and Braxton waited patiently for a response. He did not have to wait long before Holmes spoke up.

'There are features of this case that interest me,' he remarked quietly. 'You wish me to investigate the death of Kartz? Perhaps a trip to Cairo may help lift a veil that has so far covered my eyes? I suppose it is not inconceivable it is in Egypt, rather than in London, we should begin our search.' He turned to Braxton. 'Are there any other points of interest you have yet to share, regarding the dig site?'

Lord Braxton nodded. 'Since Kartz's death, there have been many thefts of similar valuables. The details of his death are the most important, but I would be grateful if you would also turn your exceptional talent to solving these thefts too. I am convinced these instances are connected, but I shall leave you to make up your own mind upon that subject. Will you go?'

The sixth Earl of Braxton looked with pleading eyes at Holmes. I found myself willing him to accept also, for I had a great wish to visit Egypt and the tombs of ancient kings myself. Perhaps all the talk of that proud civilisation had burned the need into my brain, and that of my friend, too, for it was not too long a wait that had him nodding.

Lord Braxton clapped his hands in pure delight. 'Excellent! I shall fund your expedition. Just tell me what you need, in terms of money and expenses. No, sir, I insist. You shall not spend a penny of your own money whilst this mystery remains unsolved.'

'I shall go on one condition.'

'Well, name it.'

Holmes's eyes found mine. 'Watson joins me.'

Lord Braxton turned to me. 'But will you go?'

I agreed willingly.

'Then it is settled,' said Holmes. 'We shall need the amount written onto this paper. I suggest we catch the train to Dover in the morning. Good day, my lord. I shall wire any further information or instructions to you as soon as it is pertinent to do so. I'll leave Watson here to see you out.'

That afternoon Holmes and I packed for our journey to Egypt. I consulted a timetable I'd purchased and saw an early train would allow us to catch the first boat to France, followed by a train to Italy, and then a boat to Egypt. It would be some weeks before we returned to London, but it was a trip I relished with maximum enthusiasm.

'Holmes,' I asked, as I closed the lid on my case. 'What will be our first task be when we reach Cairo?'

'I would like to visit the Antiquities Service and speak to the man in charge there, a M. Anton Bouchard. Lord Braxton has wired the service and explained that we are coming. I have given specific instructions on what I need to see, to save us wasted time, once we arrive.'

There were many questions I wanted to ask, but ran over them in my mind instead. There were some points that didn't rightly add up, but as Holmes was not keen to furnish me with his ideas when I wanted them, I decided it was better to wait until he resolved to explain further, and not waste time asking questions I knew would not be answered.

I sat in the comfortable armchair and smoked one of my favourite cigars as Holmes darted in and out of his bedroom. I picked up my book on Egypt and began to read about the excavation of tombs.

* * *

Of our journey to Cairo, I shall provide only a brief account. Morning came quickly and it was not long before we had both eaten breakfast and journeyed to Charing Cross railway station, bound for the coast.

We took trains and sailed aboard handsome boats. During those five days of travel, Holmes spent his entire existence reading through local papers he had purchased at every stop. Throughout our journey he smoked that horrid black, pungent pipe tobacco of his profusely.

I watched with interest the many ships and cargo vessels that went about their business. As I lost myself in the vista, my mind wandered to the question of what might lay before us in Egypt. My thoughts were short-lived, however, when a signal from the watchman called my attention to the fine mesh of lights burning on the horizon. With our journey to Egypt ending, now came the hard task of starting an investigation within a foreign country.

'How do you intend to find these criminals within such an overpopulated city?' I asked, as we dined on our last day of the journey.

'By the process of scientific deduction, Watson, how else?' That was the last conversation I had with Holmes as we pulled into the port and disembarked for the train that would take us to Cairo, the capital of Egypt.

* * *

It had been an arduous day of travel. For even though evening was at hand, the heat – the temperature easily exceeded ninety degrees – remained stifling. The smoke and steam from the busy trains contributed further to our discomfort, which was by now causing irritation to my eyes and skin.

The large station was dirty and overpacked with travellers from across the world. Holmes, who had changed into a light suit and matching deerstalker travelling cap on the boat, sat on his trunk and lit a cigarette. I watched the faces of those crowding around us, to see if I could gain any useful knowledge, however there were so many my eyes soon blurred. Through a combination of the heat and journey, my head pounded, so I decided I would sit and take a drink of the water Holmes had found for us.

We did not have a long wait before an antiquated steam train arrived at our platform. We boarded the overcrowded first-class compartment. A whistle then blew, and just as the train set off, the door opened and a man dressed in a linen suit hurriedly jumped in. He steadied himself, apologising to the passengers he had almost fallen into, and walked further down the carriage. I continued watching him as he eventually found a seat.

'Splendid, Watson. You noticed our shadow, then?' Holmes said, interrupting my train of thought.

'Shadow?'

Holmes nodded. 'He has been following us since we disembarked the boat.'

'Who is it? Our Mediterranean thief?'

'Or someone he is associated with. I said before that he

48

probably had an associate. We now have evidence this may be so.'

I remembered. 'It's a gang then?'

Holmes shrugged. 'A well organised group, at the very least. I've done much to avoid showing I was aware of him, which will be undone if you continue to stare.'

He was correct, so I looked to the window. 'How did he come to follow us here?'

Holmes smiled and crossed his legs, sinking back into the chair of our carriage. 'At present I can think of only one possibility.'

'What is that?'

'The obvious one,' said Holmes, offering no further explanation.

'What should we do?' I asked, ignoring Holmes's concerns, leaning to gain a better view of the shadow. Holmes, however, pulled me back into my chair.

'Be a good fellow and sit back.'

Holmes returned his gaze ahead and I noticed a rather unpleasant look in his eyes.

'We shall watch and wait, and when the time is right, we shall learn his identity and purpose. If it's trouble he wants, Watson, then he'll find it in me.'

Not that long after a food cart arrived. In the rush, I procured two sandwiches and had my canteen filled with water. I handed a sandwich to Holmes, but he held up a hand.

'I cannot allow myself the luxury of food. Some water, yes, but the digestion process requires too much of my energies.'

Holmes fussed with his pipe as I ventured another quick look at our shadow. Whilst trying not to appear to do so, I attempted to see if it were possible to determine his motives. Holmes fell asleep for the rest of our journey, and I continued to watch until my eyes felt heavy and I too drifted off.

Later that day events took a turn. It wasn't often I would see Holmes become hesitant as to his conclusions, yet from my perspective, he did seem to be a little lost.

Chapter Five

'You have come to Egypt to exercise your grey cells?'

Cairo. A place of wonder and sadness, of beauty and devastation. I was left in confused awe over the odd juxtaposition of the ancient majestic world clashing violently with a modern one.

Our train journey came finally to a shuddering end. Holmes and I left the compartment, stepping out onto a dusty, busy platform. It was here, where the hustle and bustle of commuters go about their daily business, that I realised how laborious our task would be. Within a sea of faces, turning almost nondescript in their vast number, I had lost our shadow. He'd slipped from view and blended seamlessly into the crowd. Eventually, once we'd recovered our luggage, I gave up trying to find him.

Holmes lugged our cases with ease to the exit gate and we waited outside on the pavement, along with many others, for a method of transport to the Antiquities Service. I admit to being overwhelmed by the sheer volume of traffic, but Holmes pushed his way through a sea of bodies and somehow flagged down the Egyptian equivalent of a London cab. After some bartering, Holmes opened the door and I gave a contented sigh as I climbed in and took a seat out of the sun. In no time at all, we were on our way to the museum.

'It seems we have lost our shadow,' I said, smiling.

'That's what we were meant to think,' Holmes said.

'You don't think he's driving this cab?' I did my best not to look, yet looking all the same.

Holmes laughed and then held up a hand for silence. 'Please, Watson. I implore you. No more questions, I need to think.'

With tremendous interest, I took in the fabulous sites as we wove our way through those crowded streets. The busiest day in London did not compare to the multitude of people milling around us. The diversity of buildings amazed me. Each had its own unique style. There was an old-world dignity about Cairo that somehow, even within a desert of general untidiness, seemed never to lose its charm.

The cab made a turn and came to a stop near a colossal building. It made the British Museum seem infinitesimal by comparison. Holmes paid the driver and I removed our cases from the rear compartment. Ahead of us, a little distance from the main concourse, lay an enormous staircase that led to the museum entrance. Beyond that, displayed in glass cases, sat antiquities recovered from around the world.

Like a child with energy to spare, Holmes leapt the stairs two at a time until he'd reached the summit. I struggled with our luggage through the blistering heat until my sweat blinded me. When I'd finally reached the top and dropped the cases, I scowled at my friend who seemed oblivious to my exertions. For a man who prides himself on his observational skills, he could be blissfully ignorant.

Looking back at that day, as I turn over the notes in my book, I can honestly say for the sights that befell me, I was utterly unprepared. I had visited several museums in my lifetime, but never one as grandiose as the one in Cairo. I could hardly count the sheer number of golden artefacts moulded into spectacular treasures. Their beauty and splendour surpassed anything I'd seen in similar circumstances on previous occasions. I wandered between the glass displays, unashamed by the boyish way I must have been behaving. Holmes, I noticed, kept an eye on me. Occasionally I would see him turn to a newcomer or two, but hardly ever did his eyes travel to the marvels I had immersed myself within.

At length a boy, dressed in a porter's uniform, came and bowed before Holmes. I noticed him and the boy conversing, and when their conversation had ended, Holmes dropped something into his hand, then he came and stood beside me.

'Look at this,' I said. 'The detail of the craftsmanship is astonishing.'

'Yes, quite.' His remark was unemotional.

I looked sideways at him. 'Was the boy's information useful?'

Holmes leant on his cane and smiled at the artefact. 'Time will tell.' He then lifted his cane and rested it on his shoulder. 'If you're ready to get to the business at hand?'

I nodded and he turned, walking away. I couldn't help running my eyes over the people as I followed him.

At the reception desk, Holmes pressed a bell to attract attention from the staff. A young man of no more than twenty came to attend us. His black hair was slicked back with wax cream – a fashion, we observed, of many. Mediterranean young men. The uniform he wore, similar to that of the young porter, was as splendid as the décor. He offered a smile and gesticulated as he chatted in his quick Egyptian tongue, which I admit had been lost upon me, but was answered similarly by Holmes, who displayed yet another of his many hidden talents. Apparently, he could now speak Egyptian.

Holmes turned to me. 'I told him M. Anton Bouchard was expecting us. Now we wait.'

'What is our first plan of action?'

Holmes pulled out his cigarette case and offered me one.

'I should like to freshen up first. Then perhaps a meal? I have set in motion certain enquires, and we can do nothing until answers come from them.'

'Ah, the boy porter?'

Holmes smiled. 'Indeed. We will visit the dig site tomorrow. It is of little importance, but I know how keen you are to see this ancient chamber.' At my raised eyebrow he said, 'I admit to my own level of curiosity as well.'

I watched Holmes's eyes darting back and forth from person to person. His mind, I knew, was making observations and stringing facts together about every individual his eyes fell upon. It would not have surprised me if he spotted a few villains from London who'd come to this place to escape him. Holmes wasn't easy to mistake, even in a crowd. There were surely a few fearful people here wondering why he'd come.

'I would like to examine the body of Professor Kartz,' I said.

He nodded his approval. 'Yes. That is of significant importance. We must establish the cause of death. I recognise there will be difficulties, since we have no sway with any Egyptian authorities. And we have no idea how well the body has been preserved. But those concerns must, at least for the present, wait, since Monsieur Bouchard is coming our way.'

Anton Bouchard approached Holmes with his arms outstretched. The Frenchman had a look of delight on his heavily bearded face. He was a tall, unassuming man with neatly trimmed grey moustaches, trained in that odd fashion common to the men of France.

'*Bonjour mon cher, Monsieur Holmes.*'

Holmes kissed him on both cheeks, the French custom, and I shook him by the hand.

'*Merci, Monsieur Bouchard. Ceci est mon ami et associé, Docteur John Watson.*'

'Welcome to Cairo, *monsieur le docteur*,' he said. 'I hope the journey to Egypt was not too troublesome?'

Holmes waved a hand and M. Bouchard nodded. '*Bon.*

Now come *mes amies*, we have matters to discuss of great import!'

M. Bouchard gestured that we should follow, and he led us to a doorway some distance off.

We entered a large office chamber, which reminded me of a study from some stately room in England. Ornately decorated in styles of both Egyptian and French, it had a chaise longue and comfortable, stout seats. M. Bouchard sat behind a giant desk. Holmes and I made ourselves comfortable in the soft chairs at its front.

'They fear you, M. Holmes, eh? The criminals of your England, they fear you. When the cat is there, the little mice, they come no more to the cheese, yes?'

I could tell by his expression Holmes found M. Bouchard's comment pleasing. It took me a moment to understand what he was trying to say.

'They are feasting as we speak, *monsieur*, of that I have no doubt,' Holmes replied.

'Then we must not allow them to fatten. How long do you intend to remain in Egypt?'

'For a week, possibly longer.'

'I see. You intend to enjoy the surrounding pleasures, yes?'

Holmes smiled. 'I'm sure Watson will enjoy them for us both.'

M. Bouchard laughed. 'All work and no play, *monsieur*? You have come to Egypt to exercise your grey cells?'

Holmes nodded. 'I've set them the task of tracking down many stolen artefacts, *monsieur*.'

'Ah but, M. Holmes. *Votre tâche est impossible*! The enforcement of the law is, how shall I say it? Terrible! Not a day goes by where some matter of petty theft comes thumping onto my desk. It is often hard to gain police support in such things.'

'Did you receive my telegraph from Lord Braxton?' Holmes enquired, taking one of the French cigarettes M. Bouchard offered to us.

'*Mais oui*. I have the information you requested here.'

Holmes took the envelope from him and placed it into his pocket.

'Doctor Watson would like to examine the body of Professor Kartz, and I should like to pay a visit to the telegraph office manager. Could you arrange both?'

Holmes finished his cigarette and stood.

'But of course, *monsieur*. It would be my greatest pleasure. I shall attend to all. Now, you both are booked into *l'hôtel de Barron*. I have arranged pleasant rooms for you there. Once you are settled, perhaps we shall see you both again?'

'Soon, *monsieur*. We are most grateful for your time. By your leave, we will settle into our hotel. I bid you *au revoir*.'

Holmes and I shook M. Bouchard's hand.

'*Au revoir, Monsieur Holmes et monsieur le docteur*,' he said and Holmes and I disappeared out into the vestibule.

* * *

The Barron Hotel was an extremely well-to-do place, with a cleanliness which seemed alien in a land of sand and general unkemptness. Holmes and I freshened up and then ate a meal. When we had finished, and were relaxing, Holmes offered me one of the Calistow cigarettes he had purchased from the hotel.

'Have you seen our shadow?' I asked, trying not to look too hard at the faces of the other patrons within the restaurant. Holmes shook his head.

'We left him at the museum. I would surmise he was aware we'd spotted him. Such an adversary would be worthy enough, but I sense his purpose may not be what I'd originally deduced.'

I considered what he'd said. 'Do you mean to say he isn't against us? How come you…'

Holmes held a single finger to his lips, which silenced my question.

'It is enough that we know, for now, his intentions are not contrary to our own. I'm used to having a mystery at one end of my cases, but at both ends is far too confusing. We shall deal with our mysterious shadow friend later. For now, we must agree on my plan of action.'

The cigarette Holmes gave me was awful, and I was pleased to finish it.

'What does this plan comprise?'

'A visit to the telegraph office for me,' said he, 'and the morgue for you. I need your expert opinion. M. Bouchard will have somebody drive you when you are ready to leave.'

'Tonight?' I looked down at my plate. Had I known his intention earlier, I would have ordered a smaller meal.

'What useful data we can gather is decaying with the body as we speak.'

'Wonderful,' I intoned. Holmes opened his mouth to say something, but I waved at him. My face must have betrayed my feelings, as he smiled and sank back into his chair.

Our meal then over, I acted upon Holmes's orders with a slight grumble. True to Holmes's word, M. Bouchard had organised a driver. I settled myself inside for the ride to the morgue. It was a brief journey. Without preamble, I entered the premises and met Doctor Paul Savage, the British MD who had attended Kartz when he'd died.

Savage was a tall, thin man of impeccable dress. He greeted me a little coldly.

'Doctor Watson, isn't it? I've been expecting you. I'll take your jacket. It won't be very cool where we're heading.'

Handing my jacket over, I was annoyed by the way he slung it over his arm.

'I assume you'll want to see the body right away?'

I nodded and he led me to a storage chamber.

'What was your diagnosis?' I asked to elicit conversation from him. He gave me a sideward glance.

'Since you know already my diagnosis, I'm frankly a little disappointed you need to hear it from me directly,' Savage said and offered no further explanation.

'Heart failure, wasn't it?' I showed no emotion to the offhand way he'd dismissed my questions.

'Quite so. I'll allow you to make up your own mind, since you've taken issue with it.'

'Look, Doctor Savage. I'm following up on the information needed for my client. I intend no offence, believe me.'

'It's a little too late for that.'

I tried a different tact. 'What do you make of this curse theory?'

Doctor Savage stopped. His look was not a kind one. 'I have no time for such nonsense, and nor should you. Curses indeed.' He rolled his eyes, and then strode away.

Doctor Savage led me through a set of chambers into a clean white-tiled room, which was deep inside the morgue complex. I observed several bodies covered with white linen. The pungent chemicals could not hide the putrid smell of decaying flesh. Amongst the many odours I recognised was formic acid and aldehyde. Mixed they produced formaldehyde, which is a common enough chemical used within the environment of a morgue.

Savage led me to the table where the professor's body lay and pulled back the sheet, allowing me to view his upper torso. The body's rate of decay surprised me. Kartz's green-tinged face displayed a grotesquely contorted, twisted, manic smile.

'Given the poor state of the body, I wonder why you haven't begun a post-mortem?'

'It wasn't necessary. He died of heart failure. There was no foul play suspected, and the authorities were happy with my diagnosis. The body was being made ready for cremation when we were told to stop and get it ready for you. It's very unusual. You must have some powerful friends.'

I studied the face and moved down to the left arm. I began my search along the skin and into the underlying muscle, but the likelihood I'd find evidence to prove or disprove Savage's diagnosis of heart failure was questionable. And he knew it.

The body displayed the classic signs and symptoms, but being dead for seven days, any other signs of foul play could

57

easily be put down to its decay. Initially, I had high hopes I could discover something new, but that was quickly changed by the state I found the body in.

The mucous membranes and nail beds showed unoxygenated haematoglobulin. This cyanosis had destroyed almost all the obvious visual signs, which were masked by the body's decay. All was not lost, however, as I had noticed a few things. Kartz had bitten his tongue almost complete through. Convulsions that severe weren't typical of myocardial infarction. A typical response would be to gasp, but the contorted face meant he'd been taken by a massive convulsion at the moment of death. I could not rule a heart attack out completely. I ran through other causes that might explain a convulsion of this type in my mind. It sadly didn't help narrow things down.

I moved to the fingers of the left hand and noticed at once many were broken. Savage, who'd stuck close to me as I made my observations, was quick with an answer.

'It was necessary to break the fingers to remove a glove he'd been holding.'

'He was holding a glove that tightly?' I said.

My colleague shrugged. 'I know what you're thinking,' he said. I doubted that. 'As you're aware, heart attacks vary in their ferocity. It's probable his occurred so swiftly, in the heat of the moment, he didn't have time to let go of it.'

'And yet,' I said. 'There *was* enough time for him to bite through his tongue?'

Savage examined the opened mouth, then shrugged. 'Equally not that uncommon.'

I suspected Savage saw the inconsistency but had ignored it. As I studied the tongue, I caught the faint smell of something I didn't initially recognise.

'Chocolate,' said Savage. Again, he anticipated my question. 'Apparently, he had a sweet tooth. I found the residue on his lips and fingers of his right hand.'

'Presumably he took off his glove to select a chocolate from the box?'

'If you say so. I wasn't there,' Savage said with a sniff. 'Hardly relevant though, is it?'

I moved on from the mouth and felt around the sternum, pushing as deeply as I could. I attempted to discover the rate of heart muscle expansion but stopped after a moment. The answer left me even more uneasy.

'Aside from obvious hypoxia, there appears to be no visible signs of myocardial anoxia in this man.'

'I cannot see…'

I gave him a stern look. 'Surely an attack of this nature would enlarge at least *one* ventricle of the heart?'

Savage conceded and I returned to the lower abdomen. The bloating in his agitated internal organs gave me cause for concern, but sadly the decomposition could account for that too.

As Savage was becoming less and less helpful, I kept my conclusions to myself. When I'd finished, he kindly assisted me with a towel and water. A colleague entered and whilst they distracted him, I took a scraping of the chocolate residue from Kartz's teeth and carefully put it into one of Holmes's little white envelopes, securing it in my trouser pocket.

Savage finished his conversation and turned to me.

'Well, Doctor Watson,' he said as I finished cleaning my hands. 'Is it your intention to challenge my diagnosis?' I ignored the condescending way he'd asked and shook my head. I had no proof. The deterioration of the body and the facility's lack of modern equipment meant a post-mortem at this late stage would yield an indeterminate result. Had we been in England I felt sure I could challenge him, but here? I could never hope to do so conclusively.

'Given the contorted facial muscles that remained long after rigor mortis has ceased, it suggests a cadaveric spasm. Which would explain why he bit through his tongue? Myocardial infarction might be one of many reasons for his death.'

Doctor Savage shook his head. 'Cadaveric spasms rarely

manifest in facial muscles. You'd only expect to see that in his arms or hands.'

'Such as clutching tightly onto a glove?'

He reddened. 'Yes, well, that is one possibility.' I felt his answer was reluctant. 'But that doesn't rule out a heart attack, now, does it?'

'No, it doesn't. And without a post-mortem I suppose we shall never truly know.'

'I'm perfectly happy with my diagnosis. And if you have no further need of me?'

'I appreciate your time,' I said.

Doctor Savage handed me my coat. 'Can't say it's been much of a pleasure. I'm sure you can find your own way out.' With that, he left.

I walked back to the entrance and found my driver smoking a cigarette. At my approach, he jumped back onto his cab and hefted the reigns. I was looking forward to explaining all this to Holmes.

Chapter Six

'Powers of ancient balderdash!'

I found Holmes in the hotel's entrance and at my approach he pulled me into a secluded area, and fell into an armchair. I could tell from his expression he was in an agitated state.

'What is it?' I cried as I sat on the chair opposite.

'While you were away, I had an interesting conversation with a rather odd gentleman. And when I say interesting, what I mean is perplexing and grotesque. It has given me reason to fear for our safety.'

'Tell me,' I said.

Holmes waved to a steward and ordered us both a brandy. He refused to speak until they arrived, and once he'd settled his nerves by taking a drink, he sighed.

'I shall communicate to you, as briefly as I am able, the conversation I had with the man. His name is Marcus Abbott. He is a short man, around five feet six. He is meticulous in his grooming habits, despite the recent loss of his wife.

'"Sir! Please in the name of God, you must help me," he said, almost falling into my arms at this very spot.

'What is it, man? I said, sitting him into that chair.

"'You are Sherlock Holmes, the detective from London? Oh, please tell me you are?" I am, I said, but what troubles you so much to cause you to forget your eyeglasses?

"'I had not noticed," he said. His agitation gave way to suspicion, then he offered me a strange look. "How could you know I wore eyeglasses?" Given his agitation, I felt it necessary to provide only a brief explanation.

'You have the unattached chain from your right pocket, I told him, and you carry a white mark upon the bridge of your nose where you wear them. You also have scuff marks on your shoulders where you've miscalculated the gaps on many doorframes. Tell me, how can I be of service?

'He accepted my observations with a blurted, gurgled cry. Then said, "I believe my life is in danger." He grabbed at me. His eyes were all over the place. I couldn't tell if this was resulting from chemical use, or sheer terror.

"'My friend Jeremy Kartz's murderer is close at my heels." This got my attention. Who is this man? I asked. "Ibrahim," he said. "Ibrahim Soujez. He's evil and utterly mad. Not like any normal Egyptian rogue. He's an unscrupulous devil. I told him I'll take my concerns to the police. He didn't much care for that."

'Start your story at the beginning, I said, but it was difficult to get him to focus. He kept saying that this Egyptian was a servant of the darkness, and he could call the demons from Duat, or some such nonsense. "Since Jeremy's death, many of the artefacts he discovered have gone missing, some of them I saw in Ibrahim's study." This at least seemed worth noting.

'How can you be sure he has items from Kartz's dig? I asked. "Because I helped him pull them out of that tomb. Oh please, you must help me," and then he seemed to faint. I undid his collar and passed some brandy through his lips. When he perked up, he looked shocked to find me sitting in front of him. He mumbled an apology, refused to be drawn on any questions I asked, and denied knowing Kartz, or anyone else. I sat back, perplexed by the entire situation. He stood, and with no further word, ran off into the crowd.'

'What do you make of it?' I said.

'Very little. I do not know who this Ibrahim Soujez is, and what's most important, the name Marcus Abbott has never come up at all. He claims to have been part of the dig, but I have a list of all those with permits to work in those excavations. His name does not appear.'

'Should we be concerned by this notion of servants of darkness?'

Holmes scowled. 'No. We should treat any such notion with the contempt it deserves.'

'But surely,' I protested. 'These are superstitious people. Might we consider such powers as...'

'Powers of ancient balderdash,' he retorted hotly. 'And there's an end to it.'

Cutting me off in mid conversation annoyed me.

'If you'd let me finish, you'd find I wasn't suggesting a supernatural meaning,' I persisted. 'I was merely attempting to point out that these notions, as ridiculous as they seem to us, can drive superstitious people to dangerous heights. Should that not be a consideration?'

Holmes softened his scowl. 'A thousand pardons, Watson. You are correct.'

'What will you do now?'

Holmes sat back and pulled out his pipe. 'Smoke a little while I think.'

Holmes ordered us tea, and when it arrived, poured us both a cup. We drank the brew in silence. I noticed between his clouds of smoke that Holmes's eyes burned with an intensity I'd witnessed only once or twice before. His expression was vacant. A slight smile began edging across his face. Then his eyes focused, and it was gone. I realized he'd formed some conclusion, but I would have to wait until he was ready to explain what it was.

'Did you visit the telegraph office?' I enquired.

Holmes nodded. 'Yes, and I was pleased to find the French influence on the office. It had meticulous records. I found every telegraph Kartz had sent. From the communications to Lord Braxton to the manifest of the containers he sent Johnson at the museum. The indexes were very interesting. They gave a complete list of the cargo. There was however one telegram missing.' Holmes pulled a paper from his pocket. 'This one. It is the one Warmsley handed to me at our interview.'

'Missing from their logs?'

Holmes put the paper back into his pocket. 'There is no record of it at all. Would you kindly remind me of Johnson's description of events?'

'Hold on,' I said, and Holmes smoked furiously while I pulled out my notepad. 'Let me see... Johnson said he received a wire telling him the egg was to be cleaned and catalogued as a matter of urgency.'

'It was the one point I questioned him about directly.'

I remembered that. I felt confused. 'Was Johnson lying about it?'

'A better question would be, why did Doctor Warmsley have this telegram at all?'

I thought for a moment. 'I suppose he must have picked it up after the fuss, and kept it, thinking perhaps it might be needed as evidence?'

'Then why did he not hand it to the police? They were in attendance well before you and I.'

I had no answer.

'There are strange events occurring here. I showed the telegram to the telegraph office manager. There is no questioning him upon the matter. It was *not* sent from his office.'

'Where was it sent from?' I asked. 'Is there another telegraph office nearby?'

Holmes smiled. 'Undoubtably, but the question we should ask is, why was it necessary to receive the telegram at all?'

'You say receive and not send. You're suggesting it was faked?'

He frowned as he pulled his pipe from his mouth.

'However did you reach that conclusion?'

'It seemed obvious, since you said the telegram wasn't sent by Kartz?'

Holmes relit his pipe. 'That is true. But it doesn't follow it was faked. The telegram corroborates Johnson's story of the theft.'

I couldn't help but feel lost. 'Are you saying Johnson *is* part of this crime, or not?'

'I am saying that this telegram was the only conclusive proof this golden egg existed at all.'

'Other than our client's word?'

He gave a tight smile. 'Other than that.'

I sighed. 'This entire case gets darker by the minute.'

'You think so? I find it refreshingly clear.'

I chuckled.

Holmes then said, 'Enough of telegrams. I wish to hear about your visit to the morgue. Share your findings with me. Is it your opinion Kartz died of heart failure?'

'Without an autopsy, we won't know for certain. I can't be conclusive but, no. I don't believe that's how he died.'

'What suggested an alternative to your mind?'

I pulled out the envelope and handed it to Holmes. I could tell his interest was piqued. He studied the sample through his glass, then put it to his nose and frowned. 'Chocolate?'

'Yes. I took those scrapings from Kartz's teeth. I have a theory. For what it's worth?'

Holmes leant forward. 'Share it.'

'It is possible the professor was the victim of poisoning.'

Holmes considered this. 'And your suggestion is this poison was introduced into chocolate?'

'I believe so. The body's decomposition was advanced, and that could account for some things I observed. Savage said he had to break Kartz's fingers to remove a glove he was holding, that was what first alerted me. In my experience, those suffering a myocardial infarction rarely keep hold of anything. If a poison, such as prussic acid, was introduced into chocolate, that would account for the inconsistencies I observed. It was the last thing he ate, since it still coated his teeth.'

Holmes smiled. 'Bravo. I must congratulate you on your diligence and attention to detail. Which hand had clamped onto the glove?'

'His left.'

Holmes nodded. 'And as we know he was right-handed, that spasming is most suggestive.'

'My view is, he took off the glove and was holding it when he died.'

Holmes rubbed his chin in thought. 'A cadaveric spasm?'

'I believe so.'

'Had he bitten his tongue?'

I nodded. 'Almost completely through.'

'Your diagnosis is sound, Doctor. Prussic acid is a colourless, volatile, and extremely poisonous compound whose vapours have a bitter almond odour. Chocolate would be an ideal method of delivery. Again, I congratulate you. This really is a significant development.'

'I have another theory, if I may?' I said. Holmes lit his pipe as I articulated it. 'Warmsley said much to put our minds against Johnson. I thought it odd. The stories he told of our client having a greater knowledge than his professors were a fabrication. Here's my thought. Warmsley is our inside man. His responses to your interview seemed staged. As to the theft? Warmsley had knowledge of the egg *before* Johnson. We know the telegram came to his office first. I suspect whoever sent it, a cohort perhaps, organised Kartz's murder.'

I paused as another thought occurred. 'Lord Braxton could be convinced to order an autopsy. It might prove Kartz was killed by poison, and disprove...' I clicked my fingers. Holmes raised an eyebrow, but said nothing. 'I have it! Holmes, Savage's myocardial infarction diagnosis, that's the key.'

'You've added Doctor Savage to your list of suspects? I should warn M. Bouchard to flee for his life.' Holmes's chuckle did nothing to quash my enthusiasm.

'But don't you see? It all makes sense.'

I was onto something and I was confident.

'Savage *must* be our man here. He would be the perfect person to murder Kartz, since no one would question his diagnosis. And they didn't. Warmsley and Savage. They organised Kartz's murder so they could steal the golden egg, then they framed our client.'

'And the mysterious Mediterranean?' Holmes asked.

'Warmsley, or Gough, or some other employee,' I said. 'In disguise.'

'You certainly have thought this through. I'll grant that.'

I was full of energy. 'We should have Savage arrested and then head back to London without delay.'

Holmes clapped his hands together and laughed. 'Bravo, Watson. Bravo. You know, I have said it before, and I'll say it again. Your insights are a revelation.'

His praise filled me with joy. 'I have solved it, then?'

Holmes gave me a look which caused that joy to wane. His next words made it evaporate entirely.

'Almost everything you just said was erroneous.'

I stared at him.

'My dear fellow, I did not mean to offend you. Have I not told you once before that while you may not possess genius, your gift is to inspire it in others?'

'Perhaps,' I said indignantly, 'you should explain things in simple terms, in case I'm too stupid to comprehend.'

'Tut, tut,' he said. 'Let me ask you something. Suppose, for a moment, that there was no golden egg at all?'

'But we know there was.'

'Do we? It wasn't listed in any of the manifests sent by Kartz.'

'That is true,' I conceded.

'Quite so. And if there was no golden egg, there could be no theft, since one cannot steal that which never existed. Agreed?'

Although baffled, I nodded.

'You see how this changes things? I told you the evidence at the museum seemed too good to be true. I'm certain now that it was. Whoever sent the telegram is here. It would be impossible for Warmsley or his staff to manufacture it. And whoever poisoned Kartz, is *also* here.'

'I don't understand any of this. Our client said that he'd *seen* the egg.'

'Johnson saw what he wanted to. You have your notebook there. Remind us again what he told us upon discovering the separated artefact.'

I flipped through the pages. 'There were two communications from Kartz. The first instructed Johnson to catalogue the items and inform the various departments they could begin their own analysis.'

'Which came *with* the trove of treasure separate from the egg, yes?'

'That's correct.'

'And the second?'

'Sent via telegram with instructions to secure the egg and have it cleaned and valued.'

Holmes took in a long pull from his pipe. 'Which is then conveniently stolen, before any of those aforementioned actions can be started?'

'It could be a coincidence.' I offered.

'The odds are enormously against it being a coincidence. No, no. It had to be disposed of,' Holmes said. 'Anyone with half a brain would recognise it wasn't genuine. Let's not forget, it was inside a peculiar box with four independent locks and a padlock. Other artefacts in the manifest were of enormous value, yet were not subjected to the same level of security.'

'I admit the key and lock business did seem over complicated. But why would anyone go to all the trouble of sending a fake egg in such a heavily secured box?'

'The answer to that is simple. No one sent anything.' Holmes had a twinkle in his eyes. 'It was made in the museum.'

I laughed. 'Preposterous. How could you possibly know that?'

'We both observed the answer to that, the day I examined the room. You don't recall the spillage of plaster?'

The shattering truth was now exposed. I recalled that

spillage of plaster now, but yet at the time, it seemed un-connected. 'Good grief. Where did it go then?'

'It never left the room, Watson.'

'What? Then how did we miss it?'

Holmes smiled. 'Simplicity itself. Someone smashed it into dust and spread it across the floor. A brilliant ploy. It allowed for the addition of those perfectly distinct footprints. Do you see now?'

'Ingenious. But who?'

'Doctor Warmsley, of course.'

'So, I *was* right about Warmsley?'

Holmes nodded, then smiled. 'As I said. *Almost* everything you suggested was erroneous.'

I chuckled. 'Warmsley's assessment of Johnson's knowledge was nothing more than a way to reinforce the idea he couldn't mistake a forged item for genuine?'

'Precisely so.' Holmes beamed at me. 'If Johnson could tell a genuine artefact from a fake, this charade would have died in its infancy.'

'With no reason to call for your help. I see what you mean. But what of Doctor Savage? He *could* have murdered Kartz.'

Holmes said, 'It seems unlikely.'

'And yet, he was stubborn and unhelpful. His diagnosis too quickly made. When obvious errors were pointed out, he ignored them. As a medical man, he has a duty to be thorough. I come up with an alternative, and he could have also. Savage is hiding something.'

'It is possible he is simply attempting to safeguard his reputation? Since he has no connection to the museum, nor the dig, what would be the motive? What would Savage gain from murdering Kartz?'

I could find no answers.

'I do not dismiss your concerns, my dear friend. But from what I know of the man, he's well respected and has never come under anyone's scrutiny. I agree his diagnosis was incorrect, but perhaps that's what irks you most?'

'Perhaps.' I shook away my irritation.

'I will have someone look into his activities. Will that satisfy you?'

I smiled. 'It would.'

'Then let it be so. Now, is there anything else you wish me to explain?'

'Just one thing. Why would anybody go to so much trouble to manufacture a fake theft?'

Holmes offered a huge grin. 'The most relevant question is finally asked, and the answer is simple. To play me for a fool. And it was done perfectly.'

'I don't think I'd be too happy about that,' I remarked.

Holmes shrugged. 'I've been outfoxed by an intelligent adversary. I'm not *happy* about it, but I'm also energised by the prospects it creates. It must seem odd to hear it?'

'A little,' I admitted.

He looked out into the crowds, then slowly turned his eyes back to me. His angular face was keen and alert. 'Now, *I* am in the game. I'll discover the motive behind it all. Kartz died to keep a secret. That secret is my chief focus. Kartz was the only man who could prove the existence of this golden egg and corroborate Warmsley's assessment of Johnson. But since we can already prove these things for ourselves, we only need to know why he was murdered.'

'Then we *should* head back to London?'

'Not yet. The key to this affair lies here, in Egypt.'

'Then we should attend the dig site,' I said.

Holmes nodded in agreement. 'I shall wire Lestrade to keep an eye on Warmsley, if we're not already too late on that score. This case has developed into a complicated web of stratagems between this unknown agent who controls it, and myself. There are dark undercurrents I don't much like the feel of. We should be careful of our next steps in this case.'

'How should we proceed?' I asked.

Holmes smoked his pipe for a while before answering.

'In the morning we'll visit the telegraph office then go and see M. Bouchard. We must gain as much information as we can about these Abbott and Soujez characters. If they have any connections to the Antiquities Service, Bouchard will know.'

There entered several newcomers into the foyer. My eyes darted from person to person, and it was then I noticed a white-clad man deep within the crowds. I recognised him at once, and he must have realised, for he turned and pushed his way through a group of tourists. I jumped from my chair, but Holmes pulled me back. I looked over to see he'd vanished.

'Holmes,' I protested.

'This is not the time, Watson. It is interesting he should show himself now, and in such an obvious way. But come, we must rest. The morning is not long in coming and there will be much to do.'

He stood and straightened his shirt. 'You did well at the mortuary, my dear friend. Now, good night. We will reconvene in the morning. Don't forget to bring your revolver, there's a good chap.'

Holmes then departed.

I stayed to smoke a cigar, watching the crowds as I did. But it wasn't long before weariness set in. Exhausted, I finished the cigar and headed to my room.

Chapter Seven

'The worst events may yet lie before us.'

The following day, after a restless night with little sleep, I finally met Holmes in the entrance foyer. My friend was quiet throughout our morning walk to the telegraph office. His body language remained casual, and even though he'd reminded me to bring my revolver, he didn't display any outward sign of the dangers he'd perceived.

Holmes appeared in no hurry. As we passed along the crowded streets, where threats to us could easily have increased, he appeared more relaxed. Holmes pointed to various sights and attractions. But the wonders of those ancient monuments, in the face of the dangers, failed to excite me. Being immersed in the noisy traffic of human life, he seemed less fearful of being overheard, because it was only then that he talked candidly.

'This is a singular case,' he began, gazing at the shadows cast by the full afternoon sun on the tall buildings ahead.

He pointed to a collection of figures huddled in the shadows.

'You see them, Watson? Those men grouped within the

gloom sheltering from the relentless sun? Is it an abstract of our current situation? I fear so. When I put my mind to the chain of events in this case, I see the movements of all the players. But they resemble silhouettes behind cloth. Just like those men who assemble in the shadows, they remain nebulous.'

'As if waking from a dream? The content of it strong, but the faces are unrecognisable?'

'Exactly so,' he said.

An odd chill made me shudder, despite the warmth. I understood what Holmes had meant by his unusual speech. Not for the first time my mind wandered to the idea of a curse.

'Sometimes I wonder if there *is* a supernatural element to this case.'

'Supernatural?' he replied with a show of incredulity. 'There is nothing otherworldly about this business, Watson. If anything, it is too much of this world. It strikes me, this case is steeped in old and angry blood.'

'You have lost me,' I admitted.

'Perhaps that is because I am also lost, my dear Watson.'

'What do you mean?'

Holmes sighed again, as though feeling the weight of some vast burden, and he leaned heavily on his cane. 'A crime, Watson, is a thing of nature. Like trees, it is generated by a seed. That seed, or motive, may be greed, or revenge, or lust, or despair, or one of a hundred other things. But no matter what the crime, no matter how minor or terrible it may be, there is always this seed to generate everything that follows. The form of crime will often point back to the seed. If, for example, you discover a rich man has been murdered and whose safe has been broken into, you may assume greed was the motive, although you must not rule out other possibilities as the evidence unfolds. Do you follow?'

'Certainly.'

'But in this case, Watson, what is the seed? What is the driving force behind the perpetrators of this crime? Money? They have taken nothing of value, nor have any demands been made to any authorities. Revenge, then? All the information I have on Kartz suggests he made no significant enemies to warrant such a motive for his death. Control perhaps? There is no influence that could move the museums or the Antiquities Service to grant such power. You see my problem? A theft occurs, yet nothing of value is really taken. A man is, we believe, murdered, but the motive does not appear for revenge, money, or anything else. It's a puzzle.'

'Without a picture,' I said with a chuckle.

'Once again, you hit upon the truth. We're dealing with intellects of great subtlety. We must change our tactics, as it were, if we have any hopes of defeating them.'

I pondered on Holmes's words further and was about to suggest something of my own, when he suddenly grabbed my arm, firmly manoeuvring me towards a building to our left. He put a finger to his lips then pulled me into the doorway, opened it, and ushered me inside. Holmes led me through a small shop, and to the anger of its owner, through the rear entrance. He then took me along a path leading to an outside privy, and a channel for its waste. I struggled to keep pace with him. We turned along a narrow alleyway between two buildings and just as I caught up with him, my breathing laboured at this point, Holmes pulled me by the sleeve then pushed me into a doorway. There we waited until perhaps ten minutes had passed. Holmes remained alert and I fingered my revolver.

Although Holmes could be annoying and trying, I never questioned his senses. It wasn't long after that Holmes relaxed. Casually, he stepped out of our hiding place, beckoning with a quick wave of his hand for me to follow him.

We continued through another alleyway out to the main street and to my surprise, I found we were standing alongside the entrance to the telegraph office.

The reason he'd taken such precautions were not lost on me.

'Our shadow?' I asked.

Holmes gave a quick nod. 'We must still remain cautious,

Watson. I have bought us a little time, but it won't take him long to catch our scent again.'

The offices of the telegrapher were organised and clean. The room was decorated in styles of French and Egyptian. I observed a man operating one of the many wire-mechanised telegraphs, as Holmes and I marched in. He looked up over his gold-rimmed pince-nez and acknowledged us. Holmes waited patiently for the man to finish his work.

'Are you Holmes?' he enquired. His accent was thick, but his English was impeccable.

My friend nodded.

'I've been expecting you,' he said.

'You have, no doubt, a telegram from Scotland Yard for me?'

'Yes, and never a more cryptic one have I received.'

Holmes smiled. 'That is because I did not want anyone reading its contents.'

The operator harrumphed and handed Holmes a sheet of paper. He scanned it hurriedly, his brow furrowed.

'My thanks,' Holmes said, indicating I should follow him to a place of seclusion. Once we were out of earshot, he pointed at the paper with disgust.

'It would appear our bird has flown the nest,' he remarked.

'Which one?'

'Warmsley. Lestrade reports he hasn't been seen at the museum since the day before we left London. He's attempting to locate him now.'

'Do you think he'll succeed?'

Holmes grunted.

'You said before you didn't believe he was the brains behind things. Do you think he's been silenced?'

Holmes remained lost in thought for a moment.

'I do not know. It's a turn ·for the worst though. If Warmsley went into hiding, then he must fear we are onto something. That gives our investigation a greater urgency. And if someone silenced him, as you suggest, then that same investigative urgency must still be true. What else could prompt such an obvious turn of events?'

'Could he be on his way here?'

Holmes shook his head. 'Warmsley must know I suspect him. There is no practical reason for Warmsley to risk coming here.'

I tightened the grip on my concealed revolver. 'I suppose you're right.'

'We must deal with each event as practically as we can. We cannot investigate every disappearance in London from here. That is work for Lestrade.'

Holmes continued to read the sheet and something made him double take.

'How very interesting.' He'd become excited and agitated. 'It seems Lestrade has not been idle. He has furnished me with facts pointing to events that may add more substance to this affair.' He continued to read, muttering away to himself as he did. Whatever had caught his eye, it had excited him to a point of anxiety.

'The worst events may yet lie before us,' he then added. 'I fear this evidence has turned our case even more inexplicable.'

'Feel free to explain,' I said.

'I cannot explain things in a way that would make sense to you. Lestrade lists minor details in his otherwise useless report. But I should not be unkind because his data does help me to put certain facts into perspective.'

Holmes then sighed and rolled his eyes.

'What is it, now?'

'More irrelevances. Break-ins in shipyards. He reports a number of missing items. Oil, oranges, duck fat, dynamite, soap, whiskey...' With each word his indignation increased. 'I am sure you get the picture.'

I chuckled. 'He's just trying to be thorough, Holmes.'

'Well, what next? Lost fur coats? Missing cats? Really. As if I don't have enough things concerning me, he sends these trivialities,' he said, shaking his head.

Holmes read through the telegram a number of times. With

each pass of his eyes, his brow furrowed, and then he clicked his fingers. His frown then lifted, and a surprised look came across his lean, angular face. 'Perhaps I *was* too harsh with Lestrade!'

'He has something of value?' I enquired excitedly.

Holmes turned his eyes on me. 'Not in the information itself. But a little idea has come to my mind, Watson, and it's not a pleasant one. The pieces of our puzzle are beginning to fit together nicely. The picture, as you put it, is beginning to emerge. I remarked before there appeared to be no seed, no motive. In fact, there was an obvious one and I erred in my assumption.'

'What is it?'

Holmes allowed a smile to cross his face. 'I told you before this case is steeped in old, angry blood. It's the oldest motive there is.'

'Greed?'

'Exactly. It's possible that a crime is in contemplation that requires dormancy before it can be enacted.'

'Something connected to Kartz's murder?' I asked.

'Perhaps the motive for it? I cannot say for certain. We've uncovered a number of links in our chain of events. The manufactured theft; Professor Kartz's death; and now our journey to Egypt. We're dealing with a disciplined criminal mind. Someone who employs logic and *imagination*.'

He folded the papers and shoved them into his pocket.

'I believe we've exhausted all our avenues in Cairo. We must start out for the dig site without further delay.'

'What about M. Bouchard? Should we not visit him first?'

'There isn't time. Since we are here, a telegram will suffice.'

After Holmes had dispatched several telegrams, he led me out.

'Let us return to the hotel, make a hasty pack, and be on our way to the station.'

* * *

A few hours later we sat on the train to Asyut. From there we boarded the steamer *Carrie* for Luxor. Of the days spent together journeying south, my friend was mostly silent. Once we'd boarded *Carrie*, he'd taken to pacing the decks lost in his thoughts. A few days in, he settled, and occupied his time reading one of his books. I, being a more social creature, engaged with my fellow passengers. We would pass away our evenings playing hands of bridge and generally enjoying the companionship. As our journey progressed, it seemed a black cloud had sunk gloomily around my friend.

On the last day I stood watching the passing pleasures with a mixture of excitement and trepidation. What lay before us was any man's guess, but I fancied Sherlock Holmes had a good idea of it. That he knew more than he was prepared to explain, was certain. As was usually the case, when he fell into darker moods, there was nothing I could do to elicit any useful discussion, so I didn't even try.

The captain of our steamer informed us that Luxor wasn't far off. He pointed out the colossal figures carved from ancient stones that appeared lining the east side of the Nile. A marker for our journey's end. The corpulent obelisks and shadowy figures that lay upright and crumbled, obscured by the shades of the ruins, fascinated me. As I stared at those huge structures, now cast in eerie broken sunlight, an ominous feeling overcame me. It sent a foreboding shiver up my spine.

My heirloom pocket watch showed five o'clock as the sun began to start its slow crawl back towards the horizon. I was overjoyed as our little steamer finally pulled beside the jetty. I was struck by the calmness of my companion. Holmes and I, and the many other passengers aboard, alighted to the wood-built shack that was our station. Immediately, Holmes leapt off and disappeared into the crowd, returning momentarily and ushering me towards a shaded spot on the busy concourse.

'Here, my dear fellow,' he said with a look of regret, 'is where we must part company.'

This news shocked me. Although I have travelled much of

the world, the prospect of heading alone to the dig site gave me considerable concern.

'I admit I'm perplexed,' I said. 'Where will you go?'

In answer, Holmes reached into his pocket and pulled out a card which he handed to me.

'Doctor Andrew Montgomery?' I read.

'You are to assume that name whilst you are here. As a doctor, it should not be difficult to fall into the role. My appearance is known, since my likeness has been published many times. Do not fear. All is prepared. You will be expected.' Holmes lifted his carpetbag from the sand and smiled. 'Brave heart, Watson. I will return soon and together we can wrap up this interesting problem and make good our return to London.'

'Who will expect me?'

'A man named Slone. They have need of a doctor.'

'How have you organised all of this? And when?'

'There is no time for explanations, Watson.'

'There never is,' I said with a huff. 'How am I to get there? And when I do, am I to walk in and announce myself?' This was a little much, even for Holmes. I wish he'd taken the time to explain this to me on our boat ride.

'You will not have long to wait. A cart will soon arrive to collect you. Wait here. As to your last question. I would recommend you enter as if you owned the place,' he replied, and with a firm shake of my hand, which lingered slightly longer than normal, he melted into the crowd.

Around an hour later, when nearly all those who disembarked from the boat had moved on, I watched a cart pull into the sands nearby where I waited. A native dropped from the rickety affair and came to greet me. A toothless, perspicacious owner, with a less than desirable camel steed.

'You are Doctor Montgomery, yes?'

I nodded.

'I take you. Come. Come.'

With a practiced smile, I entered the cart while he secured my traveling bag. He climbed aboard and flicked the reigns, and we set off in a westerly direction. The cart reached a rate of speed I would not have credited our beast with. I confess my notes are sketchy at this point because I took to observe more and write less. Despite my upset, I was soon lost in the vista. The views certainly were magnificent.

A little over an hour later, we entered the Valley of the Kings.

At our destination, there lay a mismatch of tented accommodations as far as the eye could see. Local untidy folk sat huddled around fires, smoking pipes, relaxing from their heavy work. I alighted near a collection of wooden shacks and canvases.

I placed my hat on my head and watched the cart disappear towards what might have been a town in the distance. As I waited with not a friend in sight, my annoyance with Holmes reappeared.

'Is that Doctor Montgomery?'

I turned to see a thin dishevelled man some distance off waving a hat to attract my attention. He was dressed in knee-high sturdy American-styled riding boots, light-brown trousers that fanned out at his thighs, and a dirty white shirt which was open at the neck. His sleeves were rolled unevenly to the elbows, exposing the sun-kissed skin of his muscular arms. His unkempt sandy hair waved in the warm breeze. The fellow had a keen face, hardened by both the sun and his work.

He approached with a genuine smile, continually waving his hat around his face to cool off. I was mirroring this action myself, but only to deter the annoying Egyptian flies. I followed Holmes's instructions and slipped into my new Montgomery persona. I waved back, acknowledging his call.

'It is you, isn't it? Doctor Montgomery?' he said, as we finally met. 'Thank the heavens you've arrived. I can't express how pleased I am. We were all relieved when your telegram arrived. Please allow me to carry your bag, sir.' He paused. 'Oh, I'm so sorry,' he said, shaking his head. A look akin to dismay crossed his face. 'My apologies. My name is Slone. Professor James Slone.'

'The pleasure is mine. I was led to believe you had need of a doctor?'

He nodded.

'Then perhaps you'd be kind enough to escort me?'

'Absolutely. Please, follow me.'

He strode off at great pace, one I struggled to match.

Professor Slone led me to a small, neat looking tent furnished with many shelves. I noticed a quantity of labelled bottles, containing any number of antidotes and serums. At the far end, on a white linen bed, lay a young man in a delirious fever. I saw at once he had been in this precarious state for some hours.

'How long has he been feverish?' I asked, reaching for my medical bag and pulling out a thermometer.

'About six hours, give or take.'

I slid the thermometer into his mouth and took his pulse. His body temperature, whilst elevated, was not dangerously high. My diagnosis was an easy one. On the side of his neck I observed a swollen lesion, reddened and inflamed. Most likely a mosquito bite that had become infected.

'Malaria,' I said. Checking his neck and face. 'It looks as if his razor has opened the wound. It's clearly infected. He needs plenty of water. I want him to sweat as much as possible, so another blanket would help. I noticed you have a good selection of medicines. I'll give him a light sedative, then go through your inventory and we'll have him right as rain in no time.'

'I appreciate that, Doctor,' he said. Then he touched my arm. 'Some people here are saying the curse has struck again. Is that a consideration?' Slone asked ominously.

'Nonsense,' I pronounced. 'It's malaria. I'll administer iodine to the wound. Do you have someone who can look in on him and reapply it, say every three hours?'

He nodded.

'Good. Then I will check his progress later this evening.'

Slone nodded and pulled the blanket up around the delirious young man. The care he displayed, and the worried looks he gave the poor man, suggested there existed a strong bond between them.

'You are found of this young man?' I asked.

'Yes,' he said, smiling. 'He's my little brother, Richard.'

'He'll be out of his delirium soon,' I said, and Slone looked back at me with grateful eyes.

'Thank you, Doctor. I'm much relieved. But come, you must be parched. I know I need some refreshment.'

'I certainly could use some water,' I remarked. The sweat was pouring from me.

'We have some cold lemonade too,' he said. 'Come on.'

Once I had been shown my tent, and unpacked, I cleaned up and dressed for dinner. The mess tent was close, and I headed in, observing three neatly dressed men sitting next to Slone, all awaiting the serving of dinner.

I sat at the table, where a heavily bearded serving man suggested, and watched as he expertly laid out a place setting. His meticulous placement of the cutlery seemed odd, in such an environment, but some traditions were hardly ever relaxed. Something in the way he held himself seemed familiar. I waved my concerns away and concentrated on my companions.

Professor Slone introduced us. Colonel Anthony Barker was an old solider of the empire, recently seconded to the British battalion in Egypt. Sat beside him was Reverend David Palmer, an ostentatious man with a long, thin nose and greying bushy eyebrows. He seemed neat of habit and very vocal, and I learnt, had not long arrived from England. Doctor Ernest Holbourne, a member of the British Museum and close friend of Professor Kartz, stood and shook my hand.

'Do you read fictional books, Doctor Montgomery?' asked Holbourne.

'I do from time to time,' I remarked. Holbourne looked to Palmer.

Holbourne chuckled. 'Well, you're in good company then. Our clerical friend also likes a good work of fiction.'

I raised an eyebrow.

He smiled at me. 'You think a man of God should concern himself solely with the good book, Doctor?'

'Not at all,' I said. 'I was just surprised by it.'

'I do like to read about things outside of Church matters from time to time.'

'Why wouldn't you? What books do you read?'

'Mostly crime. The tales of Sherlock Holmes are a particular favourite. Have you read any?'

I coughed to hide my surprise. 'A few.'

'What have you to say upon the subject of his cases?'

The question had me red faced. I attempted to cover my sudden angst by taking a drink of my water.

'Well,' I said, relaxing into my role. 'He seems, on balance, to be a bright fellow. But then, he might be a very dull unintelligent one too,' I said, quickly, 'since we only have the author's view to go on.'

Palmer allowed a smile to cross his face, and was about to make a further comment, when the server tripped, and dropped the contents of the bowl he was carrying over my jacket.

'The bloody man has dropped soup all over you,' said the colonel, red faced and rising from his chair.

I reached for a napkin and wiped the residue off my sleeve. 'No harm was done,' I said in my best conciliatory voice, attempting to save the poor server from the old soldier's wrath. 'Honestly, Colonel, it was just an accident.'

Colonel Barker narrowed his eyes at the man, but at my insistence, he let out a breath and sat down.

'A thousand apologies,' said the Egyptian. Again, I noticed something in his voice.

'Think nothing of it,' I replied. 'The jacket was old and in need of cleaning anyway.'

He bowed. 'You are too kind, I'm sure. I will have the jacket cleaned immediately after you finish here.' With another apology, he quietly walked away.

'Well,' Palmer said. 'What do you make of that? The man must have beetles in his eyes.'

The other guests laughed, except for Barker, who I noticed eyed the poor fellow as he left the room. A collection of Egyptian men then came in and served our meals.

'Reverend Palmer is a theorist, like Mr Holmes,' said Doctor Holbourne.

Palmer smiled and pointed a fork at him. 'I have a theory regarding those extraordinary cases of Sherlock Holmes.'

Holbourne chuckled as Palmer continued through mouthfuls of stew.

'Would you like to hear my theory, Doctor Montgomery?' I nodded.

'It is much as you alluded to before. Watson is the genius behind the success of Sherlock Holmes. He covers this by publicising his works in his own pen, under his friend's name.'

The conjecture, whilst ridiculous, did make me laugh. Palmer looked a little put out by my response.

'You have a theory of your own then, Montgomery?' asked Professor Slone.

'It strikes me,' I replied, 'there must be any number of public journals, court information and so forth, to corroborate Holmes's intellect?'

Palmer snorted. 'The man's a charlatan. A busybody, and that's final. His cases are works of fiction by a well-educated man. I've seen things like this before. It is to Watson we must look for the genius. The spark of intelligence is there, and not this Holmes character, if he even exists at all.'

With our meal completed, we moved onto cigars and brandy. My jacket was taken, which considering the heat I had no complaints, and we whiled the evening away with a few games of whist. Professor Slone left us shortly after our cigars, and I finished off my brandy. Once the evening had passed and the other guests had left for their respective tents, I met up with Slone and we both visited with his brother. The young man had made a remarkable improvement.

After I'd performed my medical duties, Slone led me to my tent. Weariness descended upon me and I was grateful when I could finally slip into my bed. Sleep however did not come for some time. The conversations of the evening made me worry for my old friend. I wondered where he was and what his current line of enquiry might be. But it wasn't too long before I expunged even those concerns as I fell into restful slumber.

Chapter Eight

'Above all... do not enter the tomb alone.'

I awoke bright and early the following morning, with my first thoughts on Richard Slone. As I stepped out of my tent, I was unprepared for the splendid view stretching out for miles before me. The whole valley, situated about three miles to the west of Luxor, rests on the opposite bank of the Nile River. The entire vista comprises two valleys. An eastern wadi, the Valley of the Kings proper, and a western annexe, Wadyein or, as it is more commonly referred to, West Valley. Professor Slone explained that the first king buried in the necropolis was Tuthmosis. It is said that with few exceptions, almost every king of the New Kingdom was prepared for burial within its confines.

Fastening my necktie, I made the journey to the tent of young Slone and found him much recovered. I administered another small dose of iodine onto his bite, which had subsided during the night, and helped him with the tonic I prepared the night before. After a brief conversation, Richard explained he was a student who came to assist his brother as part of a university scheme that would last for most of summer. With his strength returning, I happily engaged him upon several topics. When one of the serving Egyptians entered, the same fellow who had spilt soup down my jacket the previous night, I left him to rest.

As I exited, we locked eyes with each other, but he quickly dropped his gaze. The hair on the back of my neck lifted. For reasons I could not explain I made a hasty exit and escaped the confines of that tent.

My walk took me to the edge of the camp, and it was there I met up with Slone and Palmer. Both men greeted me warmly.

'Ah, there you are, Doctor Montgomery,' said Palmer excitedly. I observed, when he became animated in conversation, he unconsciously twisted his rosary around his right fingers. Perhaps Holmes's influence had something to do with it, for I couldn't help but drop my eyes for a moment to his knees. It was obvious, from their distinct shine, that he prayed regularly. 'Professor Slone is taking me on a tour of the dig. Pray come with us, Doctor. Oh, please say you will?'

'I confess to a degree of curiosity, so yes. That would be splendid.'

The old reverend clapped his hands in sheer delight. 'Marvellous!' he shouted. 'Simply, marvellous. Then we can both see what it is this brilliant man has been digging up.'

Professor Slone seemed embarrassed by Palmer's adulation but consented to take us both. After a brief visit with his brother, we met up at the mess tent, and followed him towards a waiting native who made the camels ready for our use. With assistance, we mounted them and our native guide rode alongside. Slone pointed and we were soon on our way.

There are many wonders in this world, but none so oddly entrancing as those I witnessed that day. I must admit, there were questions forming in my mind. The foremost one that perplexed me was the identity of the Egyptian serving man. His ability to avoid my direct gaze and make me feel uncomfortable was taking up far too much of my thoughts. There was something undeniably peculiar about the man, and I questioned my host about his background.

'He's the brother to the head of our Egyptian staff,' Slone said, as I matched his pace alongside. 'I know nothing much about him, but his references were good.'

'Can you tell me when he arrived?'

'I can't be sure. It wasn't too long ago. These men move from job to job frequently. The comings and goings of locals is not something I have a hand in dealing with. Like I said, he has family working with us. Most of them do. Is there a problem?'

'Not at all,' I said, shaking my head. 'It is just curiosity.'

'I don't know how you can tell them all apart, honestly,' the reverend said, which annoyed me.

'Why would you say something like that?' I asked.

Slone chuckled but remained quiet.

'Does it offend you? I see it does. Well, well. They are not much better than savages, really.'

'The tolerance of the church hard at work?' I said.

'Now, now, Doctor. I wasn't trying to be offensive. But you have to admit most of these people aren't educated, and there's a lot of inbreeding. Stands to reason they'd all look similar.'

I caught Slone's sideways look and said no more. Bigotry at breakfast always turned my mood sour.

'If you need more information about the man, I suggest you talk to his brother,' Slone said, as I looked to the horizon.

'That won't be necessary,' I remarked.

'Look,' Slone said. 'Up there on that ridge, you see those great stones?'

I shielded my eyes from the morning sun. 'Yes, I see them.'

'That's where we're heading. We should reach the top in about twenty minutes. We'll leave the camels in Akhmad's hands and go inside the tomb. Then we'll return for breakfast.'

He kicked his camel and we all trotted after him.

I spent the next twenty minutes in contemplation. It was now clear, since Slone had filled in the missing information I needed, why the familiarity of this serving man had impacted me. I have a reputation for not always seeing the obvious, even when it's right in front of me. And yet now, with the certainty of someone who knows the sun will rise each morning, I decided the only answer that fit was the fellow must be Holmes in disguise. Knowing this relieved and annoyed me. I would of course be careful not to upset his plans and continue as if I knew nothing. In this instance, it would be easy to do, since Holmes had not thought it necessary to take me into his confidence. Still, my annoyance at his departure hadn't lessened. His subsequent resurfacing however, did fill me with a little cheer.

The professor turned his camel across the slopes, down into the well-trodden path, and led us to the rocky area he'd pointed out earlier. We each dismounted, and the young native, Akhmad, took our camels into his practised hands, and we departed.

It was a short walk to the dig site. Professor Slone gave us a lecture on the history of the area as we went. I was very interested in his account, but it struck me that Palmer had quite a short attention span. His eyes wandered frequently around the area, including, I might add, to a group of young girls assisting a group of local men with drinking water.

'We're fairly certain the last king interred in the Valley was Ramesses the Tenth. Under his successor, Ramesses the Eleventh, they began dismantling the royal burial ground. This was because the riches were proving an irresistible temptation for thieves. Sadly, a lot of the tombs' furniture was broken up and reused. They stripped most of the occupants of their jewels and re-interred them elsewhere.'

I listened with fascination and professional curiosity as Slone continued to impart his knowledge.

'Still, the lure of buried treasure was, and still is, the motivation for all who come here to dig,' he said with a sigh. 'More often than not, the need to find objects of value blinds archaeologists to the academic data we try to gather from important burial furniture the ancient civilisations leave behind. These days, it's becoming more common to find valuable artefacts in private collections. And the sad truth is, we must look to our fellow academics and not native thieves, as many would have us believe. Not all, mind you. Kartz was interested in the history, mostly. For all its colourful character and beauty, the story of excavations in the Valley of the Kings is a sorry one.'

His eyes brimmed and he hastily rubbed the evidence of his sad recall away.

I was about to comment on Kartz's death, when Palmer suddenly put a hand on his arm.

'We feel your loss,' he said, with such conviction that I felt a pang of regret for my earlier opinion of him. 'Come sir,' Palmer said, attempting to lift Slone's mood. 'Work is the best antidote to sorrow. I see we are near the mouth of a great tomb. Tell us all. Yes. Please, tell us all.'

With a dash he was off down the dusty slope, beckoning for us to follow. Professor Slone laughed and wandered down to join him at the bottom. I reached into my pocket for my cigarette case and discovered a sheet of paper wrapped carefully around it. As I unfolded it, I was overjoyed to find a letter in my old friend's hand. I lit a cigarette and read the note.

My dear Watson,

You are no doubt wondering why I left without giving reason or cause? I apologise, but there wasn't time to give you the explanations you deserved. On our journey, I had time to ponder on a few of the conundrums I have no answers for. By mere happenstance, a possibility presented itself which necessitated my immediate journey into town. I will continue a line of enquiry there and you must gather what knowledge you can at the dig.

I am convinced the person who murdered Professor Kartz is with you. Be alert at all times, and above all, my dear fellow, do not enter the tomb alone.

Sherlock Holmes.

I read through the note three times. My deductions regarding the servant were clearly wrong. Since Holmes was some miles east of the Valley, there could be no possibility of him being this native in disguise. I have written frequently that Holmes only explained his thoughts when he'd organised them in his mind. Without outwardly expressing it, I recognised I'd often been through my share of his well-played strategies. Most, as I recall, ended in my chagrin. Still, I would follow his instructions. My misgivings about the server must surely be an indication I'd spotted the villain Holmes was referring to. He certainly had the look of someone who might like to play a long game.

'Come along, Doctor,' Palmer called out. I folded Holmes's note and slipped it back into my pocket. When he had written it, I could not answer. Considering the time needed, it occurred to me he could only have done so on the boat. His intention to leave me here was not a last-minute decision. Not for the first time I wished he'd been more forthcoming with me.

'Coming,' I said, finishing the cigarette.

Slone and Palmer were talking at length about the ruins, and with a heavier heart, I made my way down the dune to join them.

The tomb entrance was dark. Both Palmer and I descended the ancient stairs with torches, following behind the professor. When we'd reached the first plaster wall, which had been partly removed, Slone pointed out the seal embossed upon the surface. He took the torch from me, so I could get a better look. The lower impressions were much clearer. With instruction from Slone, we were able with little difficulty to make out the hieroglyphs embossed upon it.

We followed Slone as he clambered into an antechamber. We all stood utterly dumbstruck. Carefully, slowly, both Palmer and I moved between boxes of ancient treasures. All had been neatly labelled with numbers. My annoyance at Holmes evaporated. As cliché as it must seem, I could not believe what my eyes were seeing. There were so many artefacts – not all of which were made of gold or looked to be of significant monetary value – it took time for me to comprehend just what I was seeing.

'Kartz shipped a lot of the more valuable artefacts to the British Museum, although he really ought not to have. Our permits allowing us to dig are clear. All items found on Egyptian soil are property of the Egyptian government and therefore regulated by the Antiquities Service. He got around it by keeping a less than accurate catalogue and some careful sleight of hand.'

'But when someone discovers a tomb, don't the Antiquities Service send an observer, to make sure that doesn't happen?' Palmer asked.

'Yes, but as I told you before. Things at dig sites don't always get recorded properly. Sometimes archaeologists find ways around the rules. Let me show you something. You see this section of the wall?' He pointed to plaster that had been chipped away on one side. 'This is exactly what I mean. Do you see anything different about this section at the back?'

He held the flame forward.

'Oh, yes. It appears the plaster on this side is slightly darker,' Palmer said.

'And if I pull the torch back?'

'There's barely any visual difference,' I replied.

Slone nodded. 'They opened and then resealed the wall.'

I understood. 'Is that so they could remove the items before an observer arrived?'

'Indeed. A practice Kartz indorsed. It was the one thing we quarrelled about. He didn't trust the Antiquities Service. It's no secret a black market exists for wealthy collectors. He had many items of value removed before an observer arrived to oversee the cataloguing of them.'

Looking around the chamber I noticed beneath a large couch on the west wall, a partially opened entrance. It led to a second chamber. The professor referred to this as the annexe. An area of stamped plaster between two guardian statues, standing against the north wall of the antechamber, marked the entrance to a third. This was a crypt. We both stepped in to examine it, but before we could go any further, the crack of a gunshot reverberated around the chamber. It made us jump. Slone quickly exited, and we followed him to the staircase and ascended. I wondered what had caused someone to fire a pistol.

As we reached the top, and our eyes adjusted to the sunlight, we found Colonel Barker at the threshold. He met us with a grim face and we discovered it was he who held the fired pistol. The smoke was still visible from its barrel.

'Good God, man, what is it?' Slone asked.

The old colonel's narrowed eyes turned on us.

'Damned cults, that's what it is. I saw a few of those savages poking around at the ruin, fired off my pistol. Frightened them off. Damned savages.'

Professor Slone turned to us both. 'A particular group has plagued us to no end. The Cult of the Free, or something like that. They believe we have no business disturbing a Pharaoh's sacred tomb. Kartz had an altercation with one of them shortly before he died.'

Slone put a hand on the colonel's arm, and the old soldier patted it fondly.

'We'll see them off,' Barker said.

Colonel Barker turned towards me, an enquiring expression upon his sun-baked face. 'So, Montgomery?' His eyes then shifted to the priest. 'Palmer? You've seen the delights of the ancient then? What are your first impressions?'

Palmer mumbled something I couldn't quite hear and Barker nodded, then turned to me.

'What about you?'

'Wondrous,' I said, and meant it. Barker's grim expression eased slightly.

'A place of unquestionable beauty, eh? Flawless design, what? The old reverend is too shocked for words. Understandable, really.'

The clergyman soon found his voice.

'I find myself unable to express my feelings on the matter. I am, however, more concerned by this cult you mention. I've had my share of experiences with savages and their heretic idolisms. We should be very careful. The whimsical man will do much if he believes his cause is just. A native barbarian, more so.'

Colonel Barker snorted. 'You have nothing to fear, I assure you. When soft-nose revolver bullets fly over their heads, they run soon enough.'

'But the next time they come might they also bring others?' asked Palmer. 'In strength of numbers I fear one man and a revolver may not save us.'

Professor Slone appeared to agree with Palmer. I found the conversation disturbing.

'I think it is time for breakfast,' Barker said, then marched towards the camels. We all followed him.

Palmer surprised me when he took my arm. 'We need to watch that one, Doctor. His love of the revolver may very well get us all killed.'

Then he too shuffled away. He clutched at his cross a little more tightly than usual, as he descended to the path below.

I made my way up a sandy slope and scanned the vista of tombs and construction that were visible for miles around me. With one last look at the entrance, I met with the group and we mounted our steeds for the brief journey back to camp.

'You consider yourself a righteous man, Montgomery?' asked Colonel Barker, as his camel pushed itself up to a standing position next to mine. We trotted side by side in the camp's direction.

'Yes, I suppose I do.'

Barker nodded with approval. 'Good. All this ancient chaos reminds me of back when I was fighting with my old unit. Ah, those were good times. I've always had a fascination for the unknown, that's why I jumped at the chance to come to Egypt. Know what I mean?'

'Have you been here since the excavation started?'

'No,' he said. 'They posted me shortly after.'

'It's a shame about Professor Kartz. I hear there's been some thefts. No doubt this cult of yours?'

'Death is always difficult, but his was more profound. Poor Slone has never recovered. As to any *thefts*, I do believe it's the work of these cultists.' His eyes turned on me. 'What's your interest, anyway?'

'Purely medical, on the part of the death, and curiosity regarding the thefts,' I replied quickly.

The colonel seemed to accept this explanation, and his eyes became kind. 'There's always talk of the supernatural when you open old tombs. Curses and such like. Always will be, I'm afraid. Your average native is superstitious. Raised that way, aren't they? Not like us. If you want my opinion, Kartz died of a combination of heat, excitement, and dread.'

His words were ominous. But I felt they were said in such a way as to provoke a response. I did not, therefore, disappoint him. 'Dread? You mean because of this cult business?'

'Don't underestimate the power of a righteous man, Doctor,' Barker remarked pointedly. 'They come in small packs. Hunt at night. Steal during the day and spread their wild gossips to terrorise our innocent workers. Despite what Palmer says, they are not stupid or unintelligent people. Just a little ignorant, that's all. And there's the source of Kartz's dread. The unquenching thirst the native has for racial exclusion. Kartz knew at some point the words of this cult would reach those funding his expedition. He was sure when that happened, his funding would dry up. There are always scandals of one sort or another. People were dying. Items were disappearing. The weight of the truth killed him, and not some damnable curse.'

'I expect you're correct. In extreme cases, a man's heart can just give way altogether,' I remarked.

Barker nodded. It was obvious what I'd said had pleased him. 'Very true.'

'If you don't mind my asking, why are you here? Is it because you're handy with a revolver?'

Barker's face remained neutral. 'Something like that,' he replied.

The conversation ended when he flicked his camel's reigns and it trotted off.

Chapter Nine

'I'm a player in the game, Doctor, just as you are.'

Breakfast was a solemn occasion and there was little talking. Slone ate a small amount. I wondered if Barker's talk of cultists was still troubling him. Reverend Palmer ate with gusto, as did Colonel Barker. It was only then that I noticed we were one short.

'Where is Doctor Holbourne?' I asked as a plate of eggs was placed in front of me.

'He's gone into town on an errand,' Barker replied.

Into town? That made me wonder. Palmer interrupted my thoughts.

'So, Montgomery. Now you've seen the tomb, what is your reaction?' Palmer's eyes sparkled from the rays of the morning sun.

'As I said before,' I offered. 'It was most impressive.'

'I think the word you actually used was, wondrous.' He chuckled.

'Yes,' I replied, matching his levity. 'That too.'

Palmer then sighed and said something I thought odd.

'If it were not for the benevolence of the Lord above, I

should not have ventured into that place at all.' He sipped at his drink slowly. At my look, he gave me a smile. There was more behind it than usual, I decided. Something was distracting him. He'd been equally as vocal about the cult business too. Perhaps even the God-fearing reverend was also concerned? Should we all be? Until this point, I'd not given it much thought. It had certainly had an effect on my companions and put a dampener on the morning conversations.

Colonel Barker pushed his plate aside, lit a pipe, then picked up a newspaper from the table. His eyes fell over all of us, before they settled on the print.

During the silence that followed my mind began forming questions. Holmes being in town on his own business, it fell to me to gather the information he would invariably ask for, no matter how trivial that data might seem to me. I approached the cause of our silent collation, directing my question to Slone.

'What can you tell me about this Cult of the Free, anything?'

He looked up, exchanging a quick glance with Barker before answering. 'Not much. They're a relatively new group, so I'm led to believe. Isn't that so, Colonel?'

'Quite right. New group,' Barker said over his paper.

'Sabotage seems to be their thing, that and theft. We hear a lot of different propaganda, if you know what I mean? Kartz suggested they were comprised of disgruntled locals. The authorities seem to know little about them, or their true motives.'

'They know more than you think,' Barker said, through a cloud of smoke. 'They're just unwilling to commit any time and resource to removing them. Hence this,' he said, placing a revolver on the table.

Palmer looked at it in shock. He visibly bristled as he spoke. 'Really, Colonel. On the breakfast table?'

Poor table etiquette was something I had been used too over the years I'd spent living with Holmes. I'd often find some experiment or curiosity amongst the condiments. I fancied a day with my friend would probably turn the poor reverend's stomach completely.

The old soldier shrugged, but quietly removed it and went back to his paper.

'I seriously doubt they mean us any actual harm,' Slone said. 'I agree with Kartz. They're made up of ex-workers who've lost their billet. Probably from a dig that ran dry of funds. It happens a lot.'

Barker made a noise from his throat. 'Stuff and nonsense. These people are a fanatical band of terrorists. The sooner they're punished, the better. If you want my view…'

'I think we all know what your view is, Colonel,' Palmer said with a sigh.

'Hanging's too good for them,' continued Barker, ignoring the interruption.

When the servers poured coffee, the reverend excused himself and departed. It was not the most pleasant of breakfasts and I was happy when I too found an excuse and left.

As I exited the mess tent and took in a morning stroll, I gave consideration to what I'd learnt from my band of interesting companions. I suppose the most important thing I'd discovered was that anyone could have poisoned Professor Kartz. The means and opportunity were both there. Amongst the bottles I found in Slone's tent, I noticed bitter almond water – itself a prussic acid compound. In concentration it is lethal, but in lower strengths it is commonly found in confectionary. Hidden within the various bottles, I'd also discovered compound strychnine powder, another deadly poison. But when mixed, the chemical reaction caused by strychnine would actually neutralise the effect of the prussic acid. We sometimes use the two compounds in prescriptions to treat consumption. All I could say for sure was that prussic acid was on hand, and open to anyone.

Holmes believed Kartz was killed by someone here. But who? Using my friend's methods, I attempted to make observations and deductions as to the identity of the criminal.

Professor Slone was an easily excitable, often superstitious, man. But his fondness for Kartz was clear. Definitely ill at ease and unsuited to a leadership role, Slone had a poor grasp of the management of the workers, particularly the local ones, and I noticed he was distracted more often than not. He reminded me of swots I knew at school. Exceptional at their subjects, but easily bullied. No, I decided. Slone didn't have the necessary scheming needed to see through a murder. I could also discount his brother, since he was not in Egypt at the time of Kartz's death.

Colonel Barker, on the other hand, had the training and the dangerous strength of mind to kill. But my impression of his characteristics was less that of a murderer, and more so of a palpably loyal and principled gentleman. It should not be forgotten that Barker was also a decorated military veteran of our Empire. I fancied *if* he were to decide to kill anyone, Barker was the shoot first ask questions later type. Painstakingly filling chocolates with prussic acid was not in character at all. Barker had a genuine concern for the welfare of everyone here. His vigilance certainly made me feel safer, I could not deny that. Following this reasoning I ruled him out as well.

Doctor Holbourne had the knowledge and the nerve. However, something about his quiet demeanour and casual comportment gave me cause to think he might not have the stomach for murder. And what did he have to gain? There appeared to be no motive. His position hadn't changed because of Kartz's death, and his work had on the whole remained much as it was.

The entire thing perplexed me. Having ruled out the other three, it left Reverend Palmer and the strange Egyptian manservant. However, Palmer had arrived from England *after* Kartz's death.

Perhaps this Egyptian server was Ibrahim Soujez, whom Marcus Abbott told Holmes about? Abbott was the only person who'd directly accused anyone of murdering Kartz. But then, no one had seen or heard from him since he'd left our hotel. And there was no way of corroborating his story. He said he'd worked at the dig. Holmes wasn't convinced by that at all. When I asked Slone and Barker if they knew anyone by the name, they both denied it.

I reached my tent and spent an hour writing as much of these details as I could. When finished, I visited the younger Slone. As I made my way to his tent, I noticed the Egyptian lurking near a line of camels. I fancy his eyes were following me. When I deliberately looked towards him, he busied himself with his tasks and disappeared. It wasn't long afterwards that I reached Slone's tent. I spotted Palmer shuffling from it, and he too disappeared off into a crowd of native workers.

Slone was well on the mend. Still weak, physically, I was happy to note the colour brightening his cheeks. He smiled as I entered.

'You seem much recovered,' I said, as I took his pulse.

'I am feeling much better, thanks to you. Although I wish you would let me out of these clothes and bathe.' His condition was improving. The vitality of his youthful body was fighting the infections. Despite this, he was not completely out of the woods.

'You can bathe but take it easy. Don't stay out in the sun too long and keep up your fluid intake.'

'I promise,' he said, eager to leave the tent.

'Don't overdo it, I mean it,' I said, giving him my best serious look. 'You still need to rest for a day or so longer.'

He nodded, pulled the blanket off himself, and smiled as he stood and stretched.

'Stay wrapped up. It'll allow your body to sweat out the rest of the poison.'

Young Slone nodded, thanked me again, and then slipped out of the tent.

When I need to think, I often do so as I walk. With so much on my mind, I'd lost sight of where I had wandered and how long. I stopped and looked around, and soon realised I'd absentmindedly taken the path right up to the tomb. Although we'd been on camels that morning, it was not that long a walk. I had a canteen of water, a good walking stick, and my trusty old army revolver. I felt safe and, as I was over halfway already, continued until I reached the rocks where we'd hitched our camels up earlier.

The path towards the area of the tomb wasn't that far ahead, but I rested for a moment under the shade of the rocks, and took a long drink. The sun relentlessly beat down on me as I sat waving my hat to cool off. My old wound caused me discomfort and I began to regret the long journey, knowing I had to make it in return.

Under the shade of the rock, I continued to think. There was too much for me to formulate any coherent ideas. Had Holmes been here, I know he would have made more of what I'd seen and heard. With a sinking feeling, I realised that no matter how hard I tried to make sense of things, I was no further forward than when I'd arrived. In fact, the things seemed more incomprehensible than ever. All I could tell Holmes was I'd found prussic acid.

A shout for help by a local man broke me of my thoughts. He ran towards me red faced, waving his arms in the air. He seemed in a most distressed state. I tried to stop and calm him, but he tugged at my sleeve, pointing to one of the open tombs along the path in front of me.

'You come, please, you come,' was all he would say.

I relented to him pulling on my arm and followed up the path to the tomb. We went down the dank stairs and the coolness felt good. Inside a large chamber I found the reason for his distress. On the floor was a man trapped underneath a rock. I reached for his neck, holding my fingers on his carotid artery, and found a weak pulse. I turned to the local who'd alerted me and asked him to get help at the camp. He nodded and ran off, leaving me unsure if he really understood me or not. I attempted to free the half-buried man on my own, but the task was beyond me.

After a few minutes, movement behind alerted me. I looked up into the eyes of the Egyptian serving man. He held out a hand and helped me to my feet. When he spoke, I became astounded. His clear and concise voice held no hint of an Egyptian accent.

'My dear Doctor,' said he. 'Finally, we are alone.'

As he unwound the white headdress used to keep the sun from burning his head, I waited for the inevitable flourished disrobing. But it was at that moment my blood ran cold. As he pulled off his bushy moustache and beard, I gasped at the man who stood before me. It wasn't Holmes, even though I still held some suspicion it might have been, it was Doctor Warmsley from the British Museum.

'Surprised?' he asked.

I elected not to answer.

'Cat got your tongue, Doctor *Watson*?'

Knowing I was alone and, I suspected, with no help on the way, I found myself with few choices. It was then that I recalled Holmes's solemn warning about entering the tomb alone. My medical ethics had once again overridden his caution. I tried to casually slip my hand in my pocket, but before I could find the object of my search, Warmsley pulled out and pointed a revolver at me.

'I'll take that, if you don't mind.'

Somewhat crestfallen, I pulled out my old service revolver.

'Drop and kick it to me.'

I did as he instructed, and he slotted it into his belt.

'I thought there was something about you I recognised.' Warmsley said, 'Where is Holmes?'

'I have no idea,' I replied, truthfully. 'You couldn't have been on the boat with us, Holmes would have seen through you.'

'You're correct. I came directly here after landing in Cairo. It seemed logical you'd both end up here, although I'm disappointed that I only have the monkey, and not the organ-grinder.'

'Charming,' I said. 'Your game's up. We know all about it.'

He laughed. 'And what is it you think you know?'

'We know you manufactured the theft of the golden egg.'

He gave me a thin smile. 'Mr Holmes is an intelligent protagonist. It was assumed he'd discover that prior to leaving London. We had a secondary plan in place, but surprisingly he didn't. He's not that good then, is he?'

'You couldn't know we'd come to Egypt at all,' I said, a little annoyed.

Again, he gave me a toothy smile. 'Braxton played his part well.'

I was shocked, but tried not to show it. 'You're just one of many pawns then?' I asked.

'You say that as though I might think it disparaging but, in this organisation, being a pawn is highly lucrative.'

I read an evil purpose in his narrow eyes.

'I'm a player in the game, Doctor, just as you are.'

'And what part do you play, Warmsley? If that's even your real name.'

Warmsley hadn't finished his gloating.

'This pawn has been tasked with putting you and the meddling Holmes out of action, permanently. Your corpse will be all he finds on his return. Well, that and me. I'll be here also, waiting.'

I nodded. 'Since I'm about to die anyway, can I ask a question?'

'A last request?'

'If you like.'

He nodded. 'Ask away. One question.'

'Why was Kartz murdered?'

'Ah, a good question. And the answer is simple. He alone could corroborate the egg didn't come from the dig. My employer has a long reach, Doctor. Kartz had a loathing for the black market. It wasn't hard to sow seeds of distrust about the Antiquities Service. He held a fiercely loyal belief in British fairness. But you and I know better, don't we? We calculated he would see through the ploy and once the news from the museum reached him, it would only be a matter of time before our plans were ineffective. Since there could be no way to convince Holmes to come, should the world discover in *The Times* that those artefacts mentioned were not sent by him at all.'

I nodded. 'Thank you.'

Warmsley inclined his head. He then put his free hand into his pocket. 'Now, to business. Do you know what this is?' he asked, pulling out a syringe full of clear liquid.

'No, I do not,' I replied, a little unnerved.

'It is a prussic compound. Ah, I see you *are* aware of it.'

A bead of sweat tricked down my neck. Warmsley took a step closer and I instinctively retreated against the ancient stonewall.

'As a doctor, you will know what its effects are? At least your horrible death will be quick,' he purred. 'There is an antidote, of course, but not here. I have to tell you, Doctor Watson. I'm really looking forward to watching you die.'

He advanced towards me and I knew then that my game might be up. Still, there was one thing Warmsley didn't know. I wouldn't go down without a fight. Bracing myself against the wall, I waited for him to step closer. When he came for me, I propelled myself from the rock, lashing out with as much force as I could muster. He took my blow in the face and fell back. It startled him. He pulled the revolver on me, but a kick to his hand had it skidding away.

'Did no one tell you?' I said, breathing hard.

Warmsley had stepped back further. 'Tell me what?'

'I am also a soldier.'

I took a moment to delight in his obvious look of alarm, and then he snarled and came at me again.

With his left hand firmly holding onto the syringe, he backhanded me across the face. I fell against the wall. I turned as he tried to reach me, and landed a right hook into his face, and again he backed away. I rushed him, taking the arm with the syringe, but he savagely kneed my stomach. Winded, with no time to recover, he was on me again.

I used the wall as an anchor and pushed off, attempting a tackle to his midsection. But weariness and the exertion from my long walk in the sun overtook me. He sidestepped and landed a blow on the back of my neck which knocked me to the ground.

I kicked out and struck his knee. He yelled in surprise as he twisted and limped away. I crawled to the rocks and rose unsteadily to my feet. Before I could think, he pummelled my head into the wall. Dazed, I couldn't fight off his rough handling. He turned me to face him. I had barely any strength to fight, my breathing was laboured. Warmsley gripped my throat and pinned me against the rock wall. His strength was greater. When the first signs of anoxia occurred, I weakened more rapidly.

I saw his face edge closer and closer. He lifted the syringe to my neck and I attempted to block his arm, but he had me held too tightly across the chest. I watched that hateful hypodermic as he moved it towards my neck and prayed my death would be swift. With my consciousness slipping away, I saw those evil eyes flash.

And then he was on the floor.

My vision blurred as I slid down from the rock. I took in a lungful of breath. As the room refocused, it relieved me to find Reverend Palmer standing over Warmsley with a shovel in his hands. He dropped it and rushed towards me, loosening my necktie. My eyes blurred once more and when I refocused, I was shocked to find my old friend, Sherlock Holmes, standing before me. His clergy disguise discarded, he helped me maintain my balance as I stumbled towards a pile of rocks and sat down. I will never forget that mixture of fury and concern which passed across his lean angular face.

'A thousand apologies, my dear Watson,' he said. I noticed his look of relief as I further recovered. I stood as he turned his angry eyes onto Warmsley, who was curled up on the floor. Despite what he had planned to do to me, I still could not override my oath as a doctor. I knelt down in the sand and

Holmes helped me turn him. I shall never forget that face for as long as I live. His wide, staring eyes. The colour gone from his cheeks. He wore a look of total horror and confusion. When his eyes connected with Holmes's, he opened his mouth in shock.

'You, clever, clever… fiend.'

Warmsley's face then screwed up and he uttered a strangled cry, his body racked in convulsions. Despite all my efforts, I knew it was futile. I pulled out the syringe jutting from his abdomen. It had injected the contents when he'd fallen. With a strangled cry, he thrashed in proximal seizures. Not long after, he gurgled and fell silent. His body left in the most grotesque position I have ever seen.

We stepped away and said little. It had been a long time since I'd seen a man die so violently. Holmes followed me to the half-buried man under the rocks. With a sigh, I walked away. It was clear he had passed beyond my help as well.

Holmes put a hand on my shoulder. There was a flash of something bright as he offered me his flask. Grateful, I took a long drink of the warming brandy within.

Chapter Ten

'Freeze, Watson. If you move, we're dead.'

'Are you suitably recovered from your violent ordeal?' Holmes asked.

I was happy to see the look of regret cross his face, but admit at the moment of seeing it I could not shake my anger at having been put into such a position. It wasn't the first time I'd found myself in peril through his actions. The deliberate way he played games with my life made me consider what value at all my friendship had for him.

'Your intervention could not have been better timed,' I said.

'Indeed,' he remarked. The sideways glance he levied was a clear sign he recognised how upset I felt.

'And,' I said, raising an eyebrow. 'It seems you managed to come all the way from your visit to town. In record time too. Your powers are a marvel, Holmes.'

Holmes nodded, then sighed. 'I deserved that, my dear friend. Truly.'

'Friend?' I spat the word with a venom that surprised him. 'What friend puts another in mortal danger as you have done?

Is that to be the way of things between us? Does my life mean so little to you?'

He turned to me, putting his thin nervous fingers on each of my shoulders. I saw his look of regret deepen as his eyes found mine. 'Hardly. But your anger is justified.' His shoulders sank. 'For my part, I accept the risks of danger involved in my line of business. It is the inevitable outcome of organising things in my peculiar way. In failing to remember you've made no such commitment, I have erred. I am a blundering fool.'

My anger subsided a little. He must have seen it as I noticed the corner of his mouth lift.

'You knew Warmsley was here all along, didn't you?'

'I knew,' he said. Holmes gave my shoulders a squeeze then his hands dropped, and he clasped them behind his back as he paced.

'I expected Warmsley would make a move at some point.' He stopped pacing and turned. 'But please believe me when I say, I never suspected he would make an attempt on your life. Had you heeded my warning…'

'You seek to put the blame on me?'

'No, of course not. But you are a kind man, Watson. This poor fellow' – he gestured to the dead man under the fallen rocks – 'he paid the ultimate price to illicit that kindness.'

'Who was he?' I asked.

Holmes shrugged. 'A pawn, nothing more.'

'It's good that Warmsley is out of the picture,' I said, my anger all but gone.

'Good?' he shook his head. 'It is not good, my dear fellow. Nothing about this is good.'

'It strikes me…'

'Yes, his end to save you from yours was worth it. But we have lost something of value in the process. For you see, he was my only link to this organisation. The knowledge I need has now died with him.'

He took a sip from the brandy and handed it to me.

Holmes made a thorough search of Warmsley's body and retrieved a few items, pocketing them, then gave a vocal exclamation as he retrieved a small fragment of paper.

His smile widened. 'Well, well. Perhaps I was too quick in my analysis of the situation.'

'You found something of use then?'

He studied the paper and I noticed that spark in his eyes. It gave way to a happy exclaim. 'I *have* found something.'

'Will you not explain things to me?'

He nodded. 'It is the least I can do. Let us leave this awful place and sit in the sun. A chill has crept into my bones.'

Holmes re-affixed his disguise and I followed him out of the tomb along a path towards a great rock, where we sat.

'It's an ugly business, Watson,' he said, as he lit his pipe and blew out a cloud of smoke. 'I will tell you what I know, leaving out the information we have already discussed.' He smiled as his eyes stared at the horizon. 'You did a good job with young Slone's recovery.'

'Thank you. Actually, there was something I wanted to tell you about that.'

He nodded. 'You perhaps wish to tell me of your discovery of the prussic compound?'

'You found it yourself then, when you left Slone's tent earlier today?'

Holmes looked at me with kind eyes. 'I did. You made it easier to locate, since you'd unconsciously arranged the more dangerous compounds together on the shelf.'

I pulled out my notebook. 'I'm afraid I didn't discover much more than that. Anyone could have used it.'

'Yes. There's the ingenuity of it. They're all in on it, Watson. All of them. I believe the only person we can safely trust is Lestrade.'

'Warmsley said Braxton played a part as well.'

Holmes seemed pleased. 'As I say, all of them. Including Johnson.'

This revelation surprised me. I was thoughtful for a moment. 'A conspiracy?'

Holmes's eyes refocused on the horizon, then he turned to me. 'An apt observation.'

'And the journalist and editor at *The Times*? Are they too part of things?'

'The journalist, certainly. I congratulate you for making that link.'

'But why? Why was there a need to create such a convoluted case at all?'

'Again,' he said, 'you hit the mark. Why was it necessary for me to be out of London? That is the question. But let me tell things in my own way. Warmsley and Johnson manufactured the theft at the museum together. Johnson's job was to put himself in a position where even the police couldn't fail to suspect him. That was important. If the police didn't take the bait, then it was possible I wouldn't take the case. Braxton, we know, was sent to convince us to come to Egypt. His express reason was to investigate thefts of artefacts and, if possible, determine Kartz's cause of death. I already knew Kartz was murdered. What I could not know, until we arrived, was why and by whom. And now I do.'

I nodded. 'Warmsley explained that. Only Kartz knew the golden egg didn't exist. If the news of the theft reached him, he'd blow the entire thing.'

Holmes laughed. 'If saying it would only make it so!'

'I don't follow you. Warmsley said...'

'What? That they'd been influencing and focusing his fears about black-market concerns?'

'Exactly. Slone said so too. You were there, in that ridiculous disguise.'

Holmes took his pipe from his mouth. 'But consider what Slone actually told us. They quarrelled about Kartz removing artefacts from the tombs, prior to an observer arriving from the Antiquities Service.'

'Yes, because Kartz didn't trust them. He thought someone was selling the items on a black market. That's what Slone said.'

My friend shook his head. 'He said nothing of the kind.

Slone's words were "a black market exists for wealthy collectors." In that sentence, he was alerting us to his motive for killing his friend and mentor. We also have Braxton's information to corroborate that. He alluded to this practice as well, if you recall?'

He was right. Braxton had said they were selling items to fund the dig. I had forgotten that. But Slone? A murderer? I didn't believe it.

Holmes said, 'I do not condone it, but for a righteous man who could never prove Kartz's criminal activities, murder may have seemed his only option.'

'What? No, I won't accept that. Kartz was in every way a good—'

'Oh, my dear fellow,' he said, interrupting me. 'Kartz was selling the artefacts on the black market.'

This news stunned me. 'But… Warmsley said that they'd been feeding into Kartz's fears, and now you're saying he was actually one of them?'

'That is exactly what I am saying. His death must have caused a lot of discussion, but they found a way to use it to their advantage. There's genius in that. I am dispatched to look into the thefts and if possible, discover who killed Kartz. The emphasis on the former clearly meant the latter was their actual goal. Before they could install another to continue as Kartz had, they would need to remove the person who had stopped them, by killing him. And that was the true purpose behind sending me here. Do you see?'

'Not really. This entire thing is giving me a headache.'

'I understand that feeling,' he said, chuckling.

'You're saying that Kartz was working with Warmsley to…'

'Not Warmsley,' he said. 'It is an organisation, Watson. A criminal organisation. Of which there are many employees.'

'And Kartz is part of this same organisation? Along with Warmsley, Johnson, and Braxton?'

'Yes. A classless one. What do these men have in common in our society? Nothing. And yet, they are all part of this enterprise.'

'If I am to understand this correctly: Kartz, then, was selling artefacts for this organisation which was routed in the British Museum, correct?'

Holmes nodded. 'In so far as the facts point, I agree.'

'And Kartz was sending artefacts, right under the nose of the Antiquities Service, to this organisation so they could sell them to buyers in a black market for a considerable profit?'

'So far we remain in agreement.'

I was thoughtful for a time. 'But they have surely made a stupendous error in sending you here to investigate? Since you've uncovered the truth, they must surely know by now?'

With a great shout of joy, he clasped my shoulder. 'You have it. There is, however, one problem. I can prove nothing. All we have is hearsay, and a working theory.'

'But you can explain it to the police…'

He shook his head. 'No court could convict anyone based on what we would offer as testimony. And even if they were prepared to listen, what would that conviction be? Conspiracy to commit fraud? But what fraud? Where's the evidence? Warmsley is dead. Kartz is dead. With nothing to prove otherwise, Johnson can maintain his fictional story. So, I ask you, what do we reasonably have?'

I smiled. 'We have Slone.'

Holmes gave me a sad look. 'And what do you imagine that will do for us?'

'Well,' I said. 'Wouldn't his motive expose the conspiracy?'

'In court? I suspect so. But which court? He committed murder in Egypt, Watson. Not England. But there we run into difficulties. The Egyptian judiciary considers the case of Kartz's death closed. He died of heart failure. We could, through British influence, insist they reopen it, but what evidence do we have to warrant such urging? Aside from your expert knowledge, what do we have that conclusively proves our theory that he was murdered via poisoned chocolates?'

'The means are here. We have the prussic compound,' I retorted.

'All we have is a collection of poisons commonly found in a dig environment. And even if that was enough, you said it yourself, anyone could have gained access to it. We can hardly discredit Doctor Savage's diagnosis and hope it leads the judiciary to entertain a request to re-examine the body, now can we? Anticipating your next question, Slone's confession would not aid us. Even if we were able to organise a post-mortem, you have already explained that the body's decomposition will surely work against us.'

He was right, and I could find no fault with any of it.

'And now I think you're caught up.'

'Not quite,' I said. 'You haven't explained how you knew Warmsley would be here at all.'

'Ah, yes. Warmsley. The *only* member of this gang I was aware of. His aliases are many. Do you recall my mentioning *The Fall of Summer* at our first meeting?'

I clicked my fingers. 'That's right. I wondered what you meant by it, but it slipped my mind.'

'Yet for me it was the centre of my entire energy. I am a follower of amateur dramatics. It may surprise you to learn that I have occasionally given assistance to playwrights in their dramatizing of stories concerning crime. *The Fall of Summer* is one such play. Although the writer failed to heed my advice, hence my observation on the vagueness of the inspector's closing remarks. I knew Warmsley as the professional actor David Winslett. And he had skill, we cannot deny that. Was there anything else left to explain?'

'Our shadow?'

'That we shall leave for the time being.'

I nodded, and he stood, held out his hand, and helped me to my feet.

'Wait a minute, wait a minute,' I said. 'How did you organise your disguise and arrive here before I did?'

'Yes, of course. The *Most* Reverend Palmer. I laid out instructions for his birth with Colonel Barker in one of the telegrams I'd sent when we were in Cairo. Barker and I were in contact prior to us leaving London. Where do you think I got the information regarding Kartz's dig? Barker organised everything, including collecting you from the dock. He's a senior member of the Egyptian judiciary.'

'Oh,' I said, 'of course he is.'

We made a slow walk to the path.

'It appears we can do nothing, Holmes.'

'There are difficulties,' he agreed. 'But then, there are always difficulties.'

It wasn't long before we'd reached the rocky road that led down to the path and back to the camp. Fortunately, Holmes had the foresight to make preparations for our return journey. Akhmad was waiting with three camels. On seeing us emerge, he made them ready.

'See here,' said Holmes. 'You prefer to walk, I know, but considering your exertion perhaps we should ride back? Unless you favour the exercise?'

'Absolutely not.'

'I thought I knew my Watson.' He put a hand on my chest. 'But until it is no longer required, please refer to me as Palmer,' he cautioned. 'The good reverend may yet still be of some use.'

'You consider things unfinished here?'

'There are still loose ends.'

'I understand. There is another question I've been pondering.'

'Ask it.'

'Who do you think is behind this organisation?'

Holmes looked off into the distance. 'There are one or two players left in this game. We have not exhausted all possibilities at the museum where the nucleus of these events must surely have found form.'

'It fits with everything we know. I'm sure you'll discover who by the time we reach England,' I said. 'How much longer before we can return?'

Holmes looked kindly at me. 'Are the romantic wonders of Ancient Egypt finally lost to you?'

'Let's just say recent events have lessened my appreciation

for them.'

'Understandable,' Holmes said. 'There is no way to excuse or palliate Warmsley's homicidal deeds. I am remorseful though, for I know how excited you were about the lost kingdoms of our ancient cousins.'

'And the Pharaoh's curse,' I said.

'If you wish to believe in such things,' he remarked with a chuckle. 'But be consoled that Warmsley will affect nothing or anyone ever again. At the very least, isn't that something positive for us to cheer?'

'Opening that tomb led to these events, and too many people have died as a result. The world is better off without Warmsley, I agree. But had that tomb stayed buried would we be here at all? I don't believe there's anything supernatural about this case. It strikes me it's just about greed and the effect of it. Surely that must be the real curse?'

He nodded and continued walking. As we reached our transport, he turned. 'Well, Doctor Montgomery,' he said, slipping into his Palmer persona once again. 'It is almost time for dinner. Shall we?'

It was late afternoon when our camels knelt down to allow us to climb off. Holmes headed towards the tents and I quickly followed, my thoughts still centred on my brush with death. We said little while we navigated our way through. Holmes pointed, and it wasn't long before we reached the tent he was looking for. I followed as he weaved through the interconnecting pathways until he stopped outside and smiled. Holmes gave a quick look around, pulled open the flap, and ushered me inside.

'Well, well,' he said. 'Let us see if we cannot find something of use.'

'This is Warmsley's tent, isn't it?'

'Yes, hidden within the crowd. A perfect place from which to conduct his operation.'

I looked around as Holmes began a very detailed examination of its sparse contents. Warmsley was neat and tidy and his wants were small. There was a bed with a small chest for clothing at its end. He'd pushed a table and chair up against one side. There was a collection of five books next to an oil lamp atop it. I observed a toilet pan, washing bowls, soaps, and that was about it.

'How could a lowly serving man have a tent like this?'

'The organisation for which he works must have deep pockets indeed.'

'Warmsley said as much. They funded our expedition. I do wonder…'

He gave me that look I knew so well. 'I'm sure. But perhaps you would consent to let me conduct the rest of this examination in silence?'

I stepped aside and watched as Holmes made a very careful search. Given the lack of any items of note, it did not take Holmes long to finish.

Holmes sighed. 'As suspected, there was nothing of worth.'

'What about the paper you found on his body?'

Holmes nodded and pulled it out. 'It is part of a telegram.'

'What does it say?'

'Nothing we will be able to read…' His eyes turned to the books, and a smile spread across his face. 'What has happened to the brain God has given me?'

He dropped the paper onto the desk, and I settled beside him. His excited, nervous fingers played along the line of five books.

'An odd collection,' I said, turning my head to read the spines. 'Not what you'd consider an actor would own.'

'And yet, critical for his purposes, I fancy. We already know Warmsley was part of an organisation; it isn't difficult to comprehend why he might have a collection of almanacs, is it?'

I stared at them, then at Holmes.

'You do not see the connection? Forgive me, I thought it was obvious. They are used for constructing cyphers.'

'Ah,' I said, nodding. 'The subject of your new monograph? And from these books, are you able to work out what the telegram says?'

He nodded. 'We first have to decide which one of these volumes is our key, and then the rest will be easy.'

Holmes reached out and slipped a book from the centre of the neat collection. He frowned, as he tested its weight. When he opened it, the colour drained from his face. I watched the book fall from his hands and made a move to collect it, but his steel grip found my arm.

'Freeze, Watson. If you move, we're dead.'

I watched in mesmerised horror as the devilish looking snake slowly curled out from within the hollowed-out almanac. The viper flicked its eyes at each of us, rearing a horned head as it went, its long tongue constantly flicking out to taste the air. My eyes found Holmes, who had beads of sweat running down his neck. I did not need to ask if it was venomous. The look on Holmes's face told me everything.

We stood still, as the snake raised itself to the apex of its height. In a flash of movement, I would not have credited him for, Holmes had it by the throat and held in his outstretched arm.

'Quickly, Watson. Open that chest and see of if there is something by which we can contain him.'

I took in a shuddering breath and did as Holmes asked. Inside, I found a small velvet bag with a string attached to seal it.

'Turn it inside out, and place it on my left hand,' he commanded.

Holmes deftly slipped the bottom over the creature's head. With another quick movement he had the snake inside, sealing the aperture with the string. Only then did I see him visibly relax. He deposited the bag into the chest and closed it.

'I should have been prepared for something like that,' Holmes said.

'Are we to assume there may be more snakes inside the other books?'

He shook his head. 'That bag you found was the one Warmsley used to transport his venomous friend within. Since

I observed no other bags like it, it is safe to assume the other books are free from snakes.'

That argument didn't convince me at all. It appeared Holmes might have felt the same, since he tentatively tested the weights of each book without opening them. Eventually his posture relaxed and he pulled a book out. I held my breath as he opened it, but this one was not hollowed out.

'Let us see.' He flicked open a page and ran a finger along the text. Nodding, he went to another page, then grunted. 'This isn't hopeful,' he said. When he found another page, he snapped the book shut and took another. After the same exercise, he dropped it and pulled one of the last remaining two. This time he gave an exult of triumph.

'Here it is, Watson. It reads: All set. Send word as agreed. Two seven, if nothing heard.'

'You've cracked it,' I said, smiling.

But Holmes dropped the book, and his expression turned glum. 'It is useless.'

'How so? Surely, we need only send word as agreed.'

Holmes sighed at me. 'What word should we send?'

I thought about that. 'Well, couldn't you say everything is proceeding as planned? Or something like that?'

'There is a problem with that. Send word as agreed. As agreed, Watson. Surely this must suggest a prearranged phrase?'

'Or by an agreed date?'

'But that helps us even less. Which date should we choose?'

He was correct.

'No. I am convinced it is a prearranged phrase. It is the only method by which they can be assured of the identity of the sender.'

'Perhaps they might not assume that level of security is necessary?' I offered.

'You think so? Let us not forget, this is an organisation that put me in Egypt. It isn't a tremendous leap to consider I might discover and decode their system.'

'I suppose you're right.'

'There is also another problem.'

'Oh?' I said, feeling more defeated than ever.

'We do not know which of these four volumes to use to construct the return cypher.'

'Good point. Is there nothing at all we can learn by any of this?'

'Yes. Two seven. Does that not suggest something to your mind?'

I confess it didn't. 'It's meaningless. Those two numbers could mean anything. There's no context for them.'

'But come,' he said. 'We aren't so easily defeated, are we? Can you not think of anything they might represent?' Holmes had that characteristic twinkle in his eyes. It was annoying.

Then it came to me and I clicked my fingers. 'Of course. The cost of the rail tickets from Alexandria to Cairo,' I said. 'They were two and seven. Perhaps the prearranged word is Alexandria? Although it could also be Cairo, but that seems too obvious.'

'Bravo, Watson. Very well reasoned,' he said. 'But if I might offer an alternative suggestion? Wouldn't the second of July seem more obvious?'

I chuckled. 'And a little less convoluted. But what could that date signify?'

Holmes shrugged. 'Any number of things.' He then pulled out his pocket book. 'The second of July is a Monday.'

He seemed to brighten. 'Then we have a little under four weeks.'

'Are we to head back then?' I asked, hopeful in his answer.

Holmes put a hand on my shoulder. 'Yes. Egypt's charms have worn thin on us both. Let us first have a conversation with Colonel Barker. We will begin our return to Cairo first thing in the morning, visit M. Bouchard, and then head for home.'

Chapter Eleven

'We have a hard and dangerous night's work ahead of us.'

'Are you sure I can't persuade you to stay any longer?' Colonel Barker asked, as he poured two large glasses of brandy from the decanter.

Holmes took a sip and shook his head. 'We have a long return journey ahead of us. Scotland Yard must undoubtably have their hands full due to my extended time away from London. I suspect Watson and I will be quite busy when we return.'

'I understand, even if I'm sad to hear it,' he said, sitting. 'I appreciate all your help.' He turned to me. 'And you, Doctor. Thanks to your ministrations, young Slone has recovered. He plans to head back home in the next few days.'

This was good news. Holmes had instructed me not to discuss our case, nor any theories we had formed regarding it, so I did not mention our belief that Kartz was murdered by Slone.

Holmes leant forward. 'I assume you got what you needed from Marcus Abbott?'

'Enough to corroborate the evidence you supplied, yes.'

'Then you have enough to bag this Soujez fellow?'

'Him and the rest of his gang. We picked them all up this morning. A task we've been unsuccessful in doing for almost two years. I can't thank you enough.'

At my look of confusion, Holmes said, 'The colonel has been investigating a gang of black-market criminals. A man named Ibrahim Soujez was the leader of this band of thieves. They referred to themselves as...'

'The Cult of the Free?' I asked.

Barker laughed. 'You have it, Doctor. Damned cultists, eh? They've been plaguing digs across the Valley for years. Using fear and intimidation to scare off workers, then infiltrating those digs and stealing as many artefacts as they could get their grubby little hands on. We knew the cult business was just a front, but we'd not been able to pin it to a specific individual, until Mr Holmes stepped in.'

'And this Marcus Abbott was a player too,' I asked.

Holmes shook his head. 'He is a friend of Professor Slone. He and Slone noticed a number of thefts were occurring at regular intervals. It was Abbott who found a way into Soujez's organisation. Once he recognised lost artefacts amongst Soujez's possessions, he attempted to expose him. At my instruction, Colonel Barker removed him from sight since Soujez would, I have no doubt, have had him killed.'

'And what of Professor Slone,' I said, staring at Holmes.

'Slone is a hero, Doctor,' Barker said, slapping his thigh. 'A genuine hero. If it wasn't for him, we'd not even be aware of this gang. And soon they'll be all locked away as they should be.'

'A hero?' I remarked, raising my eyebrows at Holmes. He gave a slight shake of his head and pulled out his pipe.

'The outcome you hoped for, must now be assured?' Holmes said to Barker, blowing out his match. 'Based on what you can prove, I suspect you'll have little trouble presenting it to the magistrate.'

'At least until the next gang comes. The lure of treasure will always keep them nearby, sadly. What is left for you then? You have a case of your own to get back to?'

'Something like that,' Holmes remarked. 'We will head out first thing.'

'I will organise your travel. The boat for Asyut leaves the dock at eight.'

Holmes nodded and continued to smoke.

'It's a shame you won't be able to say your farewells to Slone and the others,' Barker said.

'I am sure you will find a suitable explanation for our disappearance?'

He nodded.

I chose not to say any more. As far as I was concerned, Slone was a murderer. I did not understand why Holmes had resolved he should simply be let off. It bothered me.

'Is there anything else I can do for you?' Barker asked.

'You can call off your shadow.'

Barker laughed loudly.

'You're a clever man, Mr Holmes. No denying that. When did you notice?'

'Almost immediately,' Holmes remarked over his pipe. 'I realised when I set a trap that our shadowy friend was not interested in harming us. I wasn't sure if he was one of your people, or Bouchard's.'

'So, you made a guess?' Barker said, winking at me.

I raised an eyebrow but remained silent.

Holmes smiled but said nothing more.

Holmes made preparations for our journey with Colonel Barker, and soon after we ate then retired to our tent. The yellow flame of the oil lamp cast strange shadows through the thick fog of Holmes's pipe smoke. Disjointed thoughts rattled through my brain, causing a distracted haze of emotions. It was taking me a significant amount of energy to straighten my feelings out. I noticed Holmes's eyes on me, and I gave him a tight smile.

'You have said very little since our meal, Watson. Forgive me for saying so, but you don't seem quite yourself.'

I shrugged. 'You often say you prefer me quiet.'

Holmes put his pipe down. 'There, now. I deduce your frustration is centred upon me. You are still turning over the events of the tomb?'

'No,' I said. 'It's not that.'

'Perhaps then you are annoyed, because you feel I have done little to ensure Slone is brought to justice for his crime?'

'Frankly, yes,' I said hotly. 'It wasn't an accident. It was premeditated. A lack of evidence should not be the reason why we fail to act. People have been hanged for far less.' I regretted my outburst the instant it left my lips, but Holmes to his credit simply nodded.

'Not all of them have been guilty.'

'I know that,' I said. My irritation, again, pushed the words out quicker than I liked. 'But still...'

'Miscarriages of justice happen frequently. Prosecution is *reliant* upon evidence. If we could just use your word upon the subject, well' – he smiled as he exhaled another great cloud – 'I imagine you'd have any number of people swinging at the end of a rope. But most would be innocent.'

'And yet...' I tried, but Holmes held up a hand.

'What we have is a theory. There is no actual proof. We do not have the hypodermic syringe that Slone used to inject the prussic compound into its method of delivery. Slone, along with others, was present at the time of Kartz's death. There is no way we can determine, amongst so many, that another or his hand did the actual deed. We don't even know what chocolates were purchased, or who purchased them. We can prove nothing. And there, I fear, is an end to it.'

I harrumphed. 'It's wrong, Holmes. And you know it.'

'I agree with you. But come, Watson. What would you have me do?'

Holmes refilled his pipe and lit it, waiting for me to answer.

'Tell someone. I don't know, Barker maybe? You're a respected enforcer of the law. He'll listen to you.'

Holmes nodded, then looked me square in the eyes. 'Why do you imagine I would not have already done so?'

I paused. Embarrassment crept across my face. I hadn't thought of that. I should have thought of that.

'I'm sorry, Holmes,' I offered.

Holmes waved a hand at me, smiled, put his pipe down on the table, and sank into his chair.

'Good night, Watson.'

I awoke the next morning to find myself alone in the tent. Holmes had organised fresh water and so I conducted my toilet. Once dressed, I checked my travel bag and smiled. My time in Egypt was not without its moments of interest, yet now, with the prospect of seeing England not far into my future, I felt a cheer I had not known since I was a much younger man.

Holmes was smoking his pipe at the breakfast table when I entered. It appeared Reverend Palmer had been completely expunged. Looking very much like his old self, dressed in a cream suit and matching travel cap, Holmes sat engaged in a travel book. He looked up as I entered.

'Good morning, there is fresh coffee and a light breakfast waiting for you. We depart in thirty minutes for the boat.'

Not long after, a cart arrived and we were on our way.

* * *

As before I don't intend to give a drawn-out narrative of our journey home. We had a very pleasant trip along the Nile River back to Asyut where we caught our train to Cairo. It was my last chance to enjoy the splendid views, and I took full advantage. Of the case, we spoke very little. Holmes relaxed considerably as our journey went on, and before long we were back in Cairo.

Holmes visited the telegraph office, and M. Bouchard, while I organised tickets for the boat train to Italy. As we closed in on the French port of Calais, I found my excitement increasing. And when dawn came, and the White Cliffs of Dover were visible on the horizon, even Holmes admitted his eagerness was growing to be surrounded by those familiar London streets once again.

After weeks of gruelling travel, I fell finally into my comfortable old chair by the fire.

'I feel as if I could sleep for a week,' I said.

Holmes, who was sitting at his writing desk, turned and nodded. 'I too feel the effects of our long journey, but you can only afford sleep for a day. Unless you do not wish to be there for the end?'

'I would not miss it, since I have shed as much sweat over it as you have.'

Holmes turned back to his desk. 'Perhaps more so.' He stood and walked to the mantel, checking his pocket watch. 'It is eleven o'clock,' he said. 'I shall leave you now to rest. I will return later this evening. Do not wait for me to eat.'

'Where are you going?'

'I have several loose threads to follow before we can bring this affair to a conclusion.'

'You promise not to act without me?' I asked.

Holmes nodded. 'You have my word.'

'Then I think I will have some coffee and a walk in the park. As tired as I am, I feel the need to take in the London air.'

Holmes entered his bedroom, then exited with his cane and top hat.

'Enjoy your walk,' he said, then departed.

Once Mrs Hudson's dinner was eaten, and the plates were cleared away, I pulled open my copy of *The Times* and relaxed into my armchair. Throughout our journey I had avoided newspapers, preferring to immerse myself in the delights of the ancient world. But as I opened the paper, the headline startled me. A sensational paragraph on page two read:

THE PHARAOH'S CURSE STRIKES AGAIN!

Another terrible blow falls on the archaeology world. It was reported in the

Egyptian press that Professor James Slone, the British archaeologist who took over the work started by Professor Kartz, after his tragic death, was found dead in his bed. It is not known exactly when this occurred, as details from the Egyptian authorities have been sparse. What we do know is, its judiciary have begun an investigation and that Colonel Anthony Barker, the Ashanti War hero, is leading it. Local reports suggest, once again, that the Pharaoh is continuing the campaign to punish all those who have desecrated his tomb. We can only speculate as to why Colonel Barker is on the case, but our British comrades must feel safer just knowing he is.

* * *

Holmes returned at around ten that evening. I immediately handed him the newspaper, and he read the report with interest.

'My, my,' he said, shaking his head. 'This is an unfortunate turn of events.'

'Do you think this organisation murdered him?'

Holmes closed the paper and retrieved a long-stemmed pipe from his rack.

'Given what we know, it's entirely possible.' He was thoughtful for a moment, as he lit his pipe. 'But then,' he said, 'we should not discount the possibility that he simply could not live with the guilt of his crime.'

'Meaning Slone chose suicide?'

'It's reasonable. Consider his position. Should Barker explain things as we know them, any investigation that must surely follow would ruin him.'

'Even if that investigation was unsuccessful?' I asked.

'Even then, the stigma of it would follow him. Slone could wave goodbye to any career advancements he may have had in archaeology, along with any further connection to his various academic circles.'

I nodded. 'And if he hadn't died, would those outcomes have been certain?'

Holmes flashed me a smile as he drew from his pipe, but

said no more.

'Tell me about your day,' I said.

Holmes extinguished the match and threw it into the grate. 'It was eventful, let me say that. I spent time with Lestrade going over my plans. He furnished me with several facts that almost completed my case. He lost Johnson, of course. Still, that is of no real concern.' Holmes smoked for a while longer. Then he leant forward, a sparkle set firmly in his eyes. 'Everything is set. The entire affair will conclude tomorrow.'

'Tomorrow is the first of July. Sunday.' I said, frowning. 'Surely you meant the day after? Monday, being the second?'

Holmes shook his head. 'I mean tomorrow.' He stood and stretched, then dropped his pipe on the mantel. 'I am all but worn out. I think I shall retire and sleep till noon. Then,' he said, his eyes unfocused, 'then, we shall see.'

He nodded and bid me goodnight.

At a little after noon, the door to Holmes's bedroom opened, and he came to the mantel to find a cigarette. Once he had one lit, he gave an exultant exhale and joined me at the table. I'd had a pot of coffee made ready, and he gratefully took the cup I poured.

'We have a few hours before we need make any preparations,' he said. 'It is a lovely day. I should very much like to take a walk and some lunch, if you are agreeable?'

I nodded.

'Splendid. I should be ready in ten minutes.'

Holmes and I walked for an hour or so, and during that time he refused to be drawn on any subject pertaining to our case. We stopped for a late afternoon lunch, as Holmes suggested we may not have time for dinner. Once the meal was over, we strolled back to our rooms.

It was almost seven o'clock when Lestrade knocked on our door and met us in the sitting room. It was a warm night, but I noticed he wore a thick black overcoat.

Holmes shook his hand. 'Have you done as I instructed?'

Lestrade nodded. 'The men are all in place, as agreed. Now, perhaps you might explain why I have twenty constables hidden around the perimeter of the British Museum on a Sunday evening?'

Holmes picked up his travel bag and oil lamp, and I checked my revolver was loaded.

'Let us move this conversation to your cab,' Holmes said, disappearing out the door.

The police cab rattled along the cobblestones out onto Oxford Street. Lestrade waited patiently for Holmes to give us an explanation. Holmes ran his eyes out at the streets, then turned to us.

'We have a hard and dangerous night's work ahead of us,' he said.

'What is it we should expect then?' Lestrade asked.

'A terrible crime has been in contemplation. One that if we bring to a successful conclusion, might be considered our most dangerous yet.'

Lestrade raised an eyebrow. 'You're not going to tell me anything, are you?'

I stifled a laugh with my glove, but Lestrade read me and growled.

Holmes put a hand on his knee. 'The game must be played out. I can tell you the crime we are about to prevent has been in the planning for some months, possibly longer. A very neat affair that I had difficulty piecing together. That is the truth of it.'

'How much danger are we in?' Lestrade asked.

'Mortal danger.'

'And what are we to do, then?'

'We shall conceal ourselves within the museum and wait. You have the nightwatchman's keys?'

He handed them over.

'Splendid. And the nightwatchmen themselves?'

'All replaced by my men, as agreed.'

Holmes sat back into his chair. 'Then we are ready.'

'But ready for what, that's what I'd like to know?' Lestrade said, sighing into his own chair. Holmes stared languidly out of the window and said nothing until we'd arrived in Great Russell Street, where he ordered the cab to stop.

'We must alight here,' he said, and opened the door.

'But, Mr Holmes,' Lestrade protested. 'The museum is over that way. Why can't the cab can take us right to it?'

'We are dealing with intelligent people, Lestrade. A police carriage pulling up at the museum on a Sunday evening might be considered a touch reckless in the face of that?'

Inspector Lestrade shrugged and instructed the cab to wait.

We followed Holmes through the side streets to an entrance on the side of the building. He unlocked and opened the door slowly. Lestrade narrowed his eyes at the shrubbery, then turned as Holmes beckoned us inside. It took a few minutes of navigating around displays and so on before Holmes waved us both down. We hid behind a small wall separating the room.

'What now,' Lestrade whispered.

'We wait.'

'For how long?'

Holmes said nothing and positioned himself so that he could keep watch on the two entrances.

My pocket watch read a little after nine o'clock when we heard a noise coming from somewhere ahead. Holmes gestured, and Lestrade and I closed the covers on our lamps. In the dark we waited. The night was clear. A beam of moonlight fell onto the centre of the room through a large window above. At length the noise increased, and came closer. Soon we saw flashes of torch light. Holmes looked to me. His eyes reflecting the moonlight. Sweat had formed on his lip. At his nod, I removed my revolver from my pocket and Lestrade mirrored me.

One of the large entrance doors opened and two men entered. It was too dark to make out who they were. One was carrying a box, the other held a torch and was pointing to various places. Their whispered conversation was not audible.

Holmes looked back at Lestrade and tapped a finger to his lips. Lestrade nodded and pulled out his whistle. Holmes then looked over at me and tapped his nose. I made myself ready.

The two men came through the beam of moonlight, and I immediately recognised them. It was our client, Johnson, and Doctor Gough, the antiquities manager. Holmes flew open his light and jumped out at them.

Both men had a started look on their faces.

'That's far enough,' Holmes shouted.

'Great Scott!' Johnson yelled. 'We're undone!'

Holmes then said, 'The game's up, *Mr* Johnson. *Now* Lestrade.'

A shrill whistle reverberated around the hall, and both men jumped as Lestrade and I stood, our revolvers trained on them both.

'Put the box down,' Holmes commanded. I could tell from his posture he was uneasy. 'Slowly.'

Gough sneered and held the box tighter. 'You have no idea what you've fallen into,' he said.

A clambering of boots was heard and an army of police constables burst through the doors behind them.

'Put the box down,' Holmes said in a calm voice. 'I won't ask again.'

Johnson turned to Gough. 'Do it,' he said.

Gough growled as he complied.

Holmes then shone his light on the box. 'Now, step back from it. Both of you. Easy now.'

Lestrade and I came beside Holmes. Our revolvers still aimed at both men.

'I must congratulate you,' Johnson said. 'You really are a marvel, Mr Holmes. We thought we had it sewn up. Well, we were wrong. I take it Warmsley is dead?'

'I'm afraid so.'

'We thought something must have happened,' Gough said. 'Since he failed to respond at the allotted time.'

'I assume you had a prearranged phrase to use in the telegram?'

Gough nodded. 'One only known to the three of us.'

'Ingenious. And a different almanac for the send and return cyphers?'

Gough looked impressed. 'Again, you have it.'

'As I suspected. You really did the job well. I must congratulate you.'

'Not well enough,' Johnson said, sighing.

Lestrade stepped forward. 'Well now, perhaps someone might decide to explain these things to me? What's this all about, eh?'

Holmes turned to him. 'Greed, Lestrade. It's simply about greed.'

The inspector frowned. 'These men planned to steal all these artefacts then?'

Holmes shook his head. 'They have been stealing artefacts from the museum for a number of years, Lestrade. A neat little racket. A black-market affair. I will explain the full details to you later. For now, know that by uncovering this enterprise, we've avoided a catastrophe of such magnitude that when it becomes public, must surely make you *Chief* Inspector.'

Lestrade looked between Holmes and the two men. 'What are you saying?'

Holmes pointed to the box. 'I believe you will find that to be your missing dynamite.'

Lestrade gasped. 'Great heavens. The shipyard robberies? I didn't realise you'd given that a moment's thought,' he said. He turned his hard eyes on the two men. 'You scoundrels planned to blow up the museum, with that?'

The two men said nothing.

'Cat got your tongue, eh? Right lads, put these two in irons, and…'

Johnson shook his head. 'There can be no question of our arrest.'

Lestrade growled and stepped forward, but at that moment, Johnson pulled out a small pistol of his own. Before any of us could react, he fired, dropping Doctor Gough and then turned the weapon to his own head and soon he too lay dead.

'My goodness,' Lestrade said. It was clear the event had shaken him.

Holmes looked down at the two dead men, poked at each with his cane, gave a long sigh then walked away.

The police took control of the scene and I followed Holmes outside. He lit two cigarettes and handed one to me.

'Are you okay, Holmes?'

Holmes smiled, but I could tell the events had affected him.

'Although it was a good night's work, I did not consider Johnson's response to my upending their plans.'

'I'm astounded by it. I don't think I've ever seen Lestrade so shocked.'

Holmes looked up at the stars. 'It is odd.'

'Odd?'

'Yes,' he said looking back at me. 'They certainly faced a lengthy prison sentence, but neither were in danger of the hangman's noose.'

'I suppose the loss of liberty for men like these was reason enough?'

'Perhaps.' Holmes tapped his cane on the floor.

'You did a remarkable thing, although how you came to solve it, I cannot even begin to imagine.'

Holmes smiled. 'And yet, despite that, all the evidence was before you. But I do not blame you for not seeing it. Is there anything you need an explanation for?'

'Yes,' I said. 'How did you know about the dynamite?'

'It was in Lestrade's telegram. Don't you remember? He listed the stolen items from the shipyards.'

I chuckled. 'Along with duck fat, and oranges, as I recall.'

'Even then, I couldn't be sure of their plan or whether these robberies had any connection to our case at all. When we decoded Warmsley's cypher, that's when all the links fell into place. I knew it would be something big.'

'But how did you know what part of the museum they'd

choose?'

Holmes flicked his cigarette into the road and leant on his stick. 'From Johnson; do you not recall what he said when he first consulted me?'

I thought hard then shook my head. 'No, I'm afraid I don't.'

'He told us that the Egyptian wing was closed for refurbishment, and the plan was…'

'To open by the second of July,' I said. 'I do remember now. You really are amazing.'

'Thank you. Given that I knew what the date in question meant, seeing it in a cypher must surely give it a bigger purpose? When you consider that the message was meant as a warning, should they not receive a response from Warmsley in their prearranged way, it suggested an end to the affair. Add to that a box of missing dynamite? Well…'

I finished my cigarette. 'Absolutely incredible, Holmes.'

'And now, my dear fellow,' he said, offering me his arm. 'Let us escape the ancient past, and immerse ourselves more fully in the present.'

We made a slow walk to the waiting carriage and were soon on our way home.

* * * *

There isn't much more for me to say about this case. Holmes suggested the idea was to destroy as much evidence in the museum as possible. Since any artefacts missing could reasonably be put down to the destruction, there was no way their black-market schemes could ever be exposed. As the two men killed themselves, rather than face trial, there was no one save Braxton who could answer any further questions.

Holmes, it was suggested, had saved perhaps many hundreds of lives. It must surely have been their intention to destroy the new Egyptian wing on its opening day.

With nothing linking the crime to anyone but the two dead

men, and since there was no evidence of anything missing, or persons other than the two dead men harmed, the police investigation was quietly closed. Inspector Lestrade thanked Holmes for all his hard work and he then went his own way.

The wealthy Lord Braxton, we discovered, had a fictitious title. Sadly, he too disappeared. Despite the efforts of my friend, we were never to see or hear from him again.

'A bold and daring case, Watson. Quite the intellectual challenge.' Holmes said, as we sat smoking cigars and drinking brandy by our fire. He pointed to my notebook.

'What have you decided to call it?'

'I think you already know the answer to that,' I said, waiting for the inevitable response.

'The Pharaoh's Curse, no doubt?'

'No,' I replied. 'The *Curse* of Pharaoh.'

Epilogue

It was a week later that Holmes and I sat in those comfortably large red-leather chairs, drinking brandy in the Diogenes Club. Mycroft Holmes swirled his glass in his hand, his eyes closed as he took in the story of our recent Egyptian adventure from his brother.

'That you were the one who brought this affair to its successful conclusion, was not in doubt, Sherlock. I could never have been convinced by Lestrade's account. Although he is a little above the average intelligence for a policeman in his position, he has neither the brains nor guile to deconstruct such a complicated set of events. And certainly not the type who could under any circumstances, bring such an affair to a reasoned and coherent conclusion.'

'And yet I feel sure he will gain notoriety from having apparently done so,' said Holmes.

'You are satisfied by its conclusion, then?' Mycroft asked, his great bulk leaning forwards.

The question seemed to cause the younger Holmes a moment of thought.

'I believe so,' he replied.

Mycroft's weight shifted as he leant further forward. 'And yet?'

Holmes chuckled. 'Some unease remains.'

'I suspected as much.' Mycroft sat back into his chair, a satisfied smile passing over his large red face.

'And what, pray tell, suggested this to you?'

'Ah, Sherlock. As always, it comes not from your triumphant elucidation, but rather the missing sheath of connecting clarity.'

'Explain that,' he said.

'I have no intention of doing so, since you fully understand my meaning. I know you,' Mycroft said, shrugging. 'You don't for a moment believe Gough had the brains to organise this operation.'

'I will not disagree with you.'

'Then perhaps you *are* ready?'

Holmes frowned. 'Ready? For what?'

'To take a step into a much larger world.'

Holmes looked between us. Mycroft sniffed as he sipped his brandy.

'How much larger should I consider the world to be, brother My?'

'That depends,' he said.

'On what?'

'On whether you have ever heard the name... Moriarty?'

THE END

* * * * *

SIR LAURENCE DIES

BONUS
FIRST 3 CHAPTERS

PROLOGUE

It was a hot day of the Last Summer, August 1914. The grounds of the Smythe estate were impeccable in their intricate horticultural design. The staff went about their duties without giving much thought to the wider issues of life outside the estate. What did it matter to them if a great war was looming over the horizon? It was all so far away. Everybody knew about it. Everybody talked about it. There was hardly any other topic of conversation. The general population were reminded, on a daily basis, that the Kaiser was evil and would be stopped, eventually.

Troubling though this news was it was hardly as important as serving tea on time, or making ready the tennis courts for when the Smythe and Gregson families needed to use them.

* * * * *

'Come on, Ellie.' Larry Gregson shouted up to the top of the house. The neatly cut lawn flexed underneath his rubber-soled tennis shoes. 'Rain won't hold off forever you know!'

Her smiling face came through the open window.

'Coming, darling.'

Captain Larry Gregson held himself with military bearing. He had a real Army look about him. In his early thirties, he was good looking, extremely approachable, gently firm with his subordinates, and beyond fair. He looked up and his lips curved into that famous smile as Anthony strolled into view carrying a tennis racket over each shoulder. Anthony, being around the same age, had an attractiveness about him that went beyond "good looks." It was often described by the older generation as boyishly handsome. He was the type of person that could easily turn heads in a crowd.

Anthony, like Larry, cut an athletic figure when playing any sport, especially tennis.

'I say, Larry,' Anthony said as he quickly made it to his tennis partner's side. 'I think it's going to be a splendid day after all.'

Larry, nodding in agreement, asked:

'You've set the court up, old boy?'

'Certainly have. Nets are all ready, need the players now!'

Ellie Gregson and Agatha Smythe finally appeared around the corner of the house. The twin girls were both wearing light summer dresses and tennis shoes. They were also carrying tennis rackets. Ellie's dress was pastel white-blue; Agatha's bright pink with yellow flowers.

'You boys better be ready, we're in very good form today!' Agatha and Ellie shared a wicked look as they slowly approached. Anthony laughed and handed Larry a racket. They waited as the girls sauntered past, and followed them to the court.

Ellie caught Larry's eye from over her shoulder and winked. A fleeting gesture, but enough to make him smile.

The court was set up pristinely. Along to one side, away from the court itself, a parasol, upright and open, in the centre of a large white summer table surrounded by matching chairs, was being attended to by a handsome young footman with a bleary eye. He busied himself preparing refreshments for the inevitable break in their game. Although he took his duties very seriously, he was a footman for General Smythe after all. He looked as though at any given moment he might simply fall asleep. Hearing the approaching party, he stood, straightened out his already immaculate uniform, and made himself ready beside the table.

As each of them passed, they acknowledged him. He made no movement at all, like a palace sentry, but on seeing Anthony, his professional manner broke somewhat and he smirked slightly. Eye contact was made for the briefest moment and Anthony simply raised an eyebrow. The footman quickly returned his eyes to where they should have been, looking out at nothing. Larry, noticing that Anthony had fallen behind, looked back. His quick eye took in the exchange and he frowned.

'You coming, old boy?'

With a wave, Anthony jogged towards the party. Larry was still frowning as he caught up.

Larry turned to Agatha. 'Where's David, Aggi?'

Agatha scoffed at him. 'Oh, he's far too busy talking to my wretched father to come out and play with us.'

Not that David ever played any games, other than lowdown ones, Larry thought. To Aggi he simply said. 'Never mind.'

'Now, now, Aggi darling.' Ellie purred. She put a well-manicured hand on her sister's arm. It was a light, fleeting touch, but enough to soften her sister's mood. 'He's keeping father indoors and not out here annoying us.'

'Well, that's certainly worth a degree of forgiveness then, I suppose,' Agatha admitted, grudgingly, but she wasn't smiling.

When they reached the court, Agatha gravitated towards Anthony. Larry shook his head.

'Not this time, Aggi.'

She looked down her nose at him. 'I'm certainly not pairing with you!'

Larry laughed. 'No, that's not what I meant. Why don't we break with tradition? Let's do boys versus girls.'

Larry handed a ball to Agatha. 'You said you were both in good form...shall we?'

Ellie and Agatha looked at each other and then smiled at exactly the same time.

Larry then flipped a coin, called, and the girls won the toss.

'I'll serve, then,' decided Aggi, and Larry and Anthony moved into position. With a wicked grin, she served the ball with force. Anthony had to move quickly but managed to return it hard. Ellie backhanded it straight to Larry. They played for thirty minutes and then stopped for a break.

'Two to us I believe,' Ellie said breathlessly. 'You're off your game, darling.'

'You beat us fair and square in that last game,' Larry replied, wiping sweat from his angular bronze-skinned face.

'You keep hold of that one,' Agatha said downing a glass of freshly squeezed orange juice.

'I will. He's my peach!' Ellie smiled a big smile at Larry and then a thought occurred to her. 'Anthony, did you get that paperwork sorted?' She refilled her glass.

'Yes thank you, Ellie. The General organised everything, he even swung me a commission! The age thing wasn't even an issue apparently. General Smythe made all the necessary calls, so that's that!'

'That's great news, Anthony. Didn't I tell you it would be fine? Anyway, it'll be good to have you alongside me.' Larry said this with great affection. 'We'll show these Germans what the British are made of!'

Anthony laughed as Ellie rolled her eyes. Agatha simply coughed to hide a laugh.

'Boys, boys!' Ellie mocked them with good humour, 'You need to learn to beat us girls at tennis first!'

'True enough,' Larry chuckled and turned back to Anthony. 'Time to show these girls, don't you think?'

'Lead on, sir!'

The game lasted almost an hour and then they broke for tea.

* * * * *

The sun was slowly setting over the family house as Larry and Ellie Gregson walked out into the garden. When they were far enough away, Ellie turned and put a hand on Larry's chest.

'Do look after him, darling, he's only a boy.'

'I will, Ellie. I won't let him out of my sight.'

She smiled at him. 'You'd better not, Larry Gregson!'

'And how is Dawson taking the news?'

'As he always does, my darling, with dignity and quiet grace.'

'Meaning he hates the idea?'

She laughed. 'He hates the idea, yes.'

'Good.'

They looked at each other for the longest time. Her pretty eyes sparkled. He leaned in for a kiss.

She put a gentle hand to his lips. 'Do come back to me, Larry.'

'I will, my love.'

They embraced.

'I promise.'

They stood together for some time, hand in hand. Two pairs of eyes were fixed on the sky. The sun disappeared behind the tree line, leaving a vibrant orange-blue sky in its wake. Eventually Ellie Gregson led her husband back to the house.

* * * * *

From a window high in the disused west wing of the house, Anthony had also been watching, unnoticed. He quietly pulled the curtain closed as the pair disappeared from his view.

Chapter One

Act One, 1934
The Boat

Doctor Pieter Straay stepped out of the restaurant's cabin onto the main deck and shuddered as a biting wind penetrated his woollen overcoat. He stretched out his tall frame, placed his fedora firmly onto his head and turned his collar upward. Straay had enjoyed a light meal and some interesting conversation for the past thirty minutes, but now he wanted to stretch his legs.

The steamer was small but comfortable. Doctor Straay had enjoyed the crossing so far, because the sea had been calm. The English expression "like a millpond" had instantly come to his mind. As he reached the stern, he looked back over the horizon with a fond smile. He was leaving his native country, although it was not always his home. New adventures awaited him in England.

Doctor Straay was a people watcher. It was never boring. It was an art. He would imagine a faded photograph. The detail missing, out of focus, just out of reach. With each new person, each different encounter, he gathered that detail. Observation and study introduced him to differing facets of the subject, fuelling his hunger for arcane and often superfluous knowledge. It increased his understanding and, in the same way that a child who is given complex puzzles to solve organises the misshapen pieces to form a picture, he used that technique to bring a person into focus. It sharpened his mind. As a boy, he had always been fascinated by the actions or reactions of adults and from childhood to adulthood, the fascination never left him. It was because of this he chose to study psychology.

There were people of all classes on the boat, mainly English, which always made for an interesting study. For some reason that even he had not yet been consciously able to fathom, he found the English to be his favourite study group. They could present, on occasion, a varying degree of idiosyncratic dynamics that could leave him both amused and appalled at the same time.

He ran his eye around a mixture of women and children, all wrapped up in woollen mufflers and hats, pointing at sea birds, oblivious to anything else around them. To one side he observed an assortment of rough looking men standing in huddles smoking clay pipes. Their conversation was hushed, with the occasional loud grunt or burst of laughter. Close by were well-dressed young men, talking politics or city based business news, each standing stiffly against the wind. The overlapping conversations flooded the air around him.

Doctor Straay turned his head slightly, his interest directed towards two women who had just wandered into view. One, over-dressed and smoking a cigarette through a fancy holder, was gesticulating flamboyantly. The other was a little on the plump side. She wore a shabby hand-knitted shawl right up to her neck. Her hat, which was more suitable for a summer wedding, sat precariously askew on top of her head. She gripped the hat with one hand and held the rail with the other. Her head nodded in agreement as she answered every question her companion spoke. Both were English. Their conversation was amusing, but utterly trivial.

'Typical really,' the well-dressed one barked. 'I mean really? It's just typical isn't it?'

'Oh yes! You're so right, Dotty, it's typical.'

'Who'd have thought anything would come of it?'

'I'm sure I couldn't say, Dotty.'

'Well, I just think the whole thing is so...?' Dotty was searching for the right word.

'Typical?' suggested her friend quickly.

'Yes! That's it exactly.' They looked at each other for a few seconds nodding. 'Typical!' they said together. Dotty laughed and the other joined in.

'She'll have to tell him, you know,' said Dotty as she attached a new cigarette to her holder and lit it in a well-practiced way.

'Oh yes, Dotty, I quite agree.'

'There'll be the most awful scandal!' Dotty said the word with a smile and a twinkle in her eye. It was clear that Dotty loved a scandal.

'Well, she did bring it on herself, didn't she?' her friend replied dutifully.

'She did,' agreed Dotty happily blowing smoke from her cigarette, which drifted back towards them both.

Her friend coughed.

Dotty ignored it.

'I said to Bernard the other night, isn't it just typical, I mean, really, one just can't express it in any other way, well can one?'

'What did he say, Dotty?'

'Well he agreed with me of course. That sort of behaviour is just so...?' Dotty looked at the other and raised an eyebrow.

'Typical, Dotty,' said the other on cue.

What did this conversation tell him about these two women? One was clearly dominant the other passive. It was also evident the dominant, Dotty, held some position in society, but hadn't always. Here was a woman not born into money or position. Her husband was probably the intellect or breadwinner, possibly both. He must be a very easily pleased man, Straay thought.

Her bearing, her manner, her speech, even her posture all indicated that she was elevated middleclass. An upper-class lady would not be called Dotty; she would be called Dorothy. Her companion may possibly have been a relative, but then he remembered that old adage, *you can choose your friends, but not your family.* He shook his head slightly and dismissed his first assessment. She had to be an old friend. Dotty was quite simply a very dull and uninteresting woman.

Now her passive friend, however, was of interest. She showed the higher intelligence of the two with her quick-witted replies and her way of anticipating what should be said, and how it should be said. Her eyes shone with an underdeveloped intelligence. Here he saw potential. If only society had encouraged such a woman as she to pursue academics. The world would be a far better place for it. He interpreted her untrained abilities as foresight, precognition even. She wore the clothes that would befit someone of her class and she wasn't trying to display anything other. She was also very faithful to her now richer friend. No one could easily tolerate such a woman unless there had been a lifelong friendship, possibly as far back as childhood. The intelligence was also shown in the fact that she was on a boat out of Holland which, given her status and class, she could not have afforded on her own. A reward maybe?

He smiled to himself. He liked her, if for no other reason than her loyalty to her irritating and shallow friend.

Straay turned his attention to a man talking to a child. He was clearly a navy man. The tattooed anchor just visible under his right cuff gave that away. The child, probably around twelve years old, was nodding politely.

'Ships are the best method of travel you know, my boy. Never go wrong with a ship. Get in an aeroplane and before you know it, a wing falls off and you'd be done for. Now, on a ship, if anything unlikely ever happened, well, you'd be fine.' To emphasise his statement, he pointed to a life raft.

'See here, these rafts will keep you safe. No such thing on an aeroplane,' he said with a touch of disgust in his voice. Even the word aeroplane was distasteful, clearly a biased man.

'Wing falls off and that's it, you're done for. No getting out. Down you go! Not for me, ships for me always, safer than an aeroplane.'

Here the boy stopped nodding. Straay observed that the boy was putting a lot of thought into his answer. It occurred to him if he were to have this conversation, he might point out the fateful last journey of the Titanic as a counter to the argument. The man would of course simply reply it was *because* of the lesson of the Titanic that boats were safer. He could picture the man saying, "Every boat has the right number of life rafts in the unlikely event that a ship goes down. Freak accidents happen, but you always have time, and you always have a life raft. No such thing on an aeroplane!" He might even suggest poor judgement on behalf of the captain or some other rhetorical answer that wasn't based on any fact, just his biased view of ships and the world.

Eventually the boy said, 'I went on an aeroplane once.'

'Oh yes,' the man said with no enthusiasm at all.

'Yes, we flew to France. I liked it. Watching the world go by, the clouds looked like cotton wool. On a boat all you can see is the sea!'

'What's wrong with the sea? Full of mystery is the sea.' He turned his attention to the ocean beside him.

'Aeroplanes are exciting!' continued the boy.

The navy man turned sharply. 'Well, you wouldn't say that if a wing fell off. You'd be done for.'

The boy changed the subject.

'Are we on the port or starboard side?' he asked.

'Port,' the man said with a smile. 'You want to know a little saying that helps you to remember it?'

'Oh yes please!' the boy answered enthusiastically.

'You know what Port is, the drink I mean?'

'You have it after dinner, don't you?' the boy seemed unsure with his answer, but the seaman nodded approvingly.

'That's the stuff. Any more of that Port *left*. That's what you say.'

The boy was, again, thoughtful. 'Anymore of that Port left?' The man nodded at him. The boy was clearly still confused but eventually he got the meaning.

'Oh, Port, *Left,* I see. That makes it much easier, thanks!'

'You're welcome, my boy. So, which is safer then, hmm? Boats or aeroplanes?' He pulled out a white crumpled bag of humbugs and playfully looked inside.

'Well...,' said the boy eyeing a humbug the man had selected and slowly popped into his mouth.

'Aeroplanes do have life jackets...' the boy said hopefully.

'They're not much use to you if a wing falls off though, are they?'

The man toyed with the sweet bag.

'True—unless you land in the sea of course,' the boy replied softly, his eyes fixed hypnotically on the bag.

'If you survive the impact,' the man said matter-of-factly as he slowly closed the bag.

'Well I guess...' The man looked down and noted with a wry smile, the boy was fully entranced by the bag of sweets.

'It has to be boats then,' the boy said firmly. The logic of his argument had been betrayed! His eyes shone brightly. It seemed that all he could think about now, was the taste of the humbugs. The man smiled a winner's smile.

'There you are, see? I was right! Boats are simply the safest method of travel. Here,' he said triumphantly. 'Have a humbug!'

Doctor Straay watched the boy enthusiastically take the boiled sweet. It had been amusing to witness the discourse. Here he saw an adult who desperately wanted a boy's approval, and couldn't get it with reason, so he had resorted to bribery to achieve his goal. It was a symptom of the times. He enjoyed observing these people converse. It didn't really matter how superficial their conversations were as long as they were happening. In a way, he felt it would always give him a reason to observe and to learn.

Straay casually lit a cigarette and slowly walked around to the starboard deck where the shade gave way to the warming sun. He manoeuvred around the two talking women, lifting his hat as he did so.

'Doctor Pieter Straay?' a voice said from behind him.

Chapter Two
An Introduction

The Dutchman looked around for the source of the voice. He quickly recovered from his initial startled reaction and smiled. He hadn't known that anyone on board knew him, and he'd told only a select handful of people his plans.

'Yes it is I, Straay, Mr...?'

The man wore a formal suit in light grey with black leather shoes and a stylish grey hat. He was in his late fifties to early sixties. The first thing that struck the doctor was the overlapping mesh of scars on the neck and left side of the man's face. His jaw was crooked on one side, his lower lip twisted awkwardly downwards, and the left cheek and muscle under his eye slightly sunken. He also had no left eyebrow. This man had clearly been in some terrible accident at some point in his early life; an accident that probably made him unrecognisable to anyone who knew him before it occurred. His bearing indicated he was a military man.

Doctor Straay had a habit, especially when presented with a person who had piqued his interest, of falling into what some of his friends would categorise as "foreign mode." He used it to disarm in some cases, and to gather information in others.

The newcomer had a cheerful nature. He removed his hat and held it to his chest as he spoke.

'Gregson,' he said. 'Laurence Gregson. Well, actually, if you want to be pedantic, Lieutenant Colonel Sir Laurence Gregson.'

'You prefer Colonel, or Sir Laurence?'

'Not sure I like either these days,' admitted Gregson with a smile. 'I used to prefer Larry, but even that seems hollow.'

'Ah but to the, hmm, how do you say it…,' he made a pretence of searching for the right word. Gregson quickly offered one.

'Unacquainted?'

'Excellent, yes unacquainted, so what would you prefer I call you?'

'Sir Laurence will do.'

'Then Sir Laurence it is, pleased to meet you.'

They shook hands.

'And I you, Doctor Straay. Psychology is your field I believe, Criminal Psychology.'

Straay raised an eyebrow. 'You are exceptionally well informed, can it be that my fame has spread further than I imagined?'

'Ah, well not quite,' he chuckled and then hastily added, 'That's not to say you aren't famous of course, I'm sure you are, in your field I mean, bound to be, it's…'

'I was teasing you, Sir Laurence.' Straay smiled, Gregson nodded once.

'Right you are. Anyway, let's just say I know someone who knows some people, who tell me things when I need to know.' He laughed at the look he was getting from the tall Dutchman.

'I'm sure you get the idea, doctor.'

'Sounds incredibly complicated.' Straay flicked the butt of his cigarette into the sea.

'Yes, it certainly can be,' admitted Sir Laurence.

'You are a member, then, of the secret service?'

'Oh good lord no! No, I'm more of a… well, let's just say, an adviser to the Home Office.' He paused for a moment. 'Got the post shortly after the war.'

Straay considered this for a moment. 'It was during the war that you had the accident?'

Sir Laurence looked puzzled for a moment, but Straay pointed to his scars.

'Oh, the face?' Sir Laurence chuckled. 'Yes, bomb blast, lucky to be alive really. Ancient history now. Well, except for the scars.'

'They remind you daily of your experiences?'

'Not really, they remind me how lucky I was. Others weren't so.'

Straay nodded. 'You were saying about the Home Office?'

'Yes, a cousin of mine is a Member of Parliament and my uncle served the Home Office during the war. I think you'll find if you go back even sixty or seventy years, you'll always find a Gregson in a Government post somewhere.'

'A family affair then?'

'Something like that,' Sir Laurence smiled.

'So you return to England from a holiday?'

'Partly. Had a nice weekend in Amsterdam though, you?'

'No, for me I travel to England for my health, also I will provide some assistance in my professional capacity. It has been too long since I was last there.' There was a sparkle in his eyes. Sir Laurence noticed.

'Busman's holiday eh? So, you're a big hotshot detective now, at least that's what I've been hearing?'

'Well yes and no.'

'That's an interesting, if cryptic response, Doctor Straay.'

That's what I was going for, he thought to himself. He checked his pockets for his cigarettes and when he found one, he said, 'Yes, truly I observe and perform crime detection, I spent some time assisting the police with their investigations around Europe and now, well I am content to perform my own investigations when the mood takes me, but not as a consulting detective like your Sherlock Holmes of fiction.'

Sir Laurence offered a match, which they both shared.

'I'm more a Christie fan myself.' He leant on the rail, cigarette dangling from his well-manicured hands. 'Oh yes, Holmes was a great detective and an interesting man written by a very clever author, but I prefer the complexity of a Christie novel.' He spoke with what appeared to be good authority.

Straay agreed with him. 'Yes, I myself favour Poirot over Holmes in the novels. In nearly all the cases of Holmes, there are always little clues no one can draw any inference from, unless they have his specific knowledge of crime, science, and the underworld. For example, the lime cream from the hair tells Holmes the villain goes to one of three barbers in one side of London, because only these three barber establishments use a certain type of wax lime cream.'

Sir Laurence nodded. 'Ah yes, his arcane knowledge wins against the police there.'

Straay took a long draw from his cigarette and continued.

'Naturally, Holmes can detect this complex mixture from one strand of hair. He can gauge a man's height and stature from his footprints, which isn't as farfetched as some people might believe. He can determine the state of the man's health from the silk band in his hat. He can tell what type of cigar the villain smokes, from an extensive ash catalogue; and let us not forget the man must also be wearing the special shaped studded boots he always wears.'

Gregson laughed heartily. 'It appears these villains only ever have one pair of shoes or boots!'

'Indeed! So then,' Straay was in full flow now. 'Holmes goes to these three barbers who are each given a description. "Well, that's Barnaby Wilson!" says the second barber. Simple, logical, and well followed out, but a little unrealistic in my opinion.'

'I agree with you.' They both flicked their cigarettes into the fast moving sea below.

Straay allowed his eyes to focus on the horizon.

'No, I prefer the psychological aspect of crime. With Poirot, I find he thinks and he acts within. For the reader, it was never about the ash, the hair, or even the body. It is about his clever brain working out the solutions to twisted puzzles. No disguises. How does she describe him? A walking brain. Although the trick with discovering the employment, method of travel and maladies and other ailments Holmes employs in many stories, I like these very much.'

Sir Laurence again laughed. 'Indeed, that's what makes the detective much more interesting. The simple crime becomes more complicated. Like the nanny who knows the family secrets and later dies. Then there's the newly introduced uncle at some fancy cocktail party just off Hyde Park. He turns out to be his brother-in-law's cousin, wanted for robbery by the Yard.'

Sir Laurence was clearly enjoying himself. As Straay pulled out another cigarette and lit it, he noted with mild interest that Sir Laurence really was a connoisseur of crime fiction.

'On the other hand,' continued Sir Laurence, 'someone who isn't known as a family member but later goes on to become the love interest of some girl, so he can secretly kill her father, then goes on to claim an inheritance that passed down the family line, which skipped a generation or two...'

Straay allowed him to continue uninterrupted. It gave him time to study.

'...or maybe a man goes to war then returns, different, bitter, and war fatigued. He goes on to establish himself in some big fancy country estate, but secretly isn't the same person who left it all those years previously. Wildly absurd but a damn good read, don't you think?'

Straay's head bobbed enthusiastically. 'Yes although in fairness, the crimes in these books are always a let-down for me.'

'How so?'

Doctor Straay sighed inwardly and thought, *how many times must I explain this position?* Through experience over the years he'd found if he didn't give an adequate answer, the general impression was he was simply being difficult, or worse, it was some form of professional snobbery.

'It must be very difficult for the writer because they have to keep us interested and if we discover the identity of the criminal too early, why bother to read on? What annoys me is this. The writer always keeps little secrets from us in order to be the revelation at the end. Now I have tried on several occasions to determine the criminal in many books, but always I am wrong, because later I'm told something by the detective, which wasn't in any of the evidence or presented in any fashion during the book prior to the dénouement.' Straay finished his cigarette and again deposited it into the sea.

'It has to be this way, I suppose,' he continued, 'otherwise we'd never say. "Well I thought she'd done it," or, "I always suspected him!" This is not always the case, of course.'

'How so?'

Straay shrugged. 'Other writers have been more careful to lay out clues along the way such as a sentence here, a remark or observation there, and so on.'

'Interesting perspective,' Sir Laurence thoughtfully remarked. 'So, you stopped enjoying the stories because you felt cheated by the author?'

'Partly, but also like anyone who works in the detection of crime, to read about it for amusement tends to be like taking your work home with you. I also find it very hard to imagine England has so many idiot policemen serving in the position of Inspector or Chief Inspector. In so many cases, the police fail to discover the criminal and the good detective, the brilliant detective, hunts them down; but in reality, the police work diligently to apprehend the criminal. They have the resources and the technology at their disposal.'

'Good point.'

'What does the detective need with scientific analysis, or blood samples, or fingerprints?' Straay said this with a half-smile.

'They have the little silver cigarette case left in the open safe with the initial AG, or JL and we know at least two people who were at the party were called Andrew Johnson or Ariadne Jenkins. So the police, convinced one or the other is guilty, ignore the warnings of our famous detective and go off to search the backgrounds to determine which one of these people are guilty. Now we have the red herring thrown in to make us believe the police have it right, because Arthur Jacobs or Adrian Jefferson was the only one who left his seat at dinner. Maybe he took a call that no one can corroborate. Maybe poor Arthur is also a confidence trickster or a jewel thief.'

'He possibly has some past criminal record,' Sir Laurence added. 'They generally do.'

'Again, an excellent point. It strengthens their case. So neatly, it all falls onto him. Now the police have their man. The detective says they have it wrong but the stalwart Inspector shakes his head. No, he says, we have all the evidence we need. Therefore poor Arthur Jacobs is now charged with the crime and as far as the police are concerned the case is closed.'

'Yes I see where you're going with this; the answer is far too obvious,' Sir Laurence said.

'Exactly so. The answer then must come by some revelation only our great detective is able to determine, with the use of the arcane knowledge he and only he possesses. He determines AJ is in fact not a name, but a secret society of hatpin makers or embroidery merchants dating back some thirty years or more. This society *must* be secret and linked to, or have been directly involved in, crimes of the past, which is how he knows all about it.'

He paused for a moment. Sir Laurence seemed to be hanging on his every word.

'It is ascertained most of these people are dead, except maybe twenty or so, and only one was at the party. *Voilà!* Arthur Jacobs is now saved! The Inspector shakes the detective by the hand and grudgingly thanks him...'

Sir Laurence laughed heartily and said, 'Bravo!'

Straay bowed slightly and then proceeded to pull out another cigarette. 'As I said, it is not easy to find pleasure in a story, when you over-analyse everything you read.'

'You've really thought that through! You should write your own story. I'm sure you'd give them all a run for their money.'

'This thought has occurred to me—'

'I imagine though,' Sir Laurence said, ignoring the remark, 'if you could turn off your brain and just read the story, it would become what it is, just a story.'

'It is true what you say, but how does one turn off the brain? Or should I say the little grey cells.'

'Not easily. I'm with you there. I wish I could turn off my own brain occasionally. Still, nothing one can do about it, so best not to dwell. How long will you be in England?'

'A little while. I'm performing some work for Scotland Yard. They have a division now open to using psychology and, as an expert in my field, I was honoured to be asked to assist.'

'You're too modest, I understand you're going to the Yard to organise and develop the unit, not just to assist.'

'You are, again, remarkably well informed, Sir Laurence.' Straay studied him a little more closely.

'I am.' He gave a rather steel-like look and then a thought occurred to him. It made him smile. 'I say, why don't you come and stay with us this weekend?'

'Well—' Straay hesitated.

'I have some interesting friends and they would definitely fit the bill for a good murder mystery!' Sir Laurence gave a mischievous grin.

'Oh? You do interest me, but—'

Sir Laurence again ignored him. 'Let me see. Well first off there's the enchanting Lady Agatha. Resourceful, intelligent but little or no common sense and utterly useless with money; probably the holder of a serious and disturbing deep secret she thinks no one else knows about.' He thought hard for a moment.

'Then there's the venerable Major Heskith. A good, honest, solid chap. A history of sound decisions and perfect record but, out of the war environment, has turned to drink. Who else? Yes… There is also the debonair Doctor Powell: family doctor, intelligent, cunning and handsome. Who knows how many bodies are locked away in his cupboard, eh?' Sir Laurence was counting off people with his fingers as he spoke.

'Oh and I mustn't forget the very loyal but equally money-grabbing lawyer, Desmond DuPont, whose friendship is predicated on the size of my chequebook! I suspect you'd find a weekend with all of these people thoroughly entertaining! You must come. It would be delightful. There might even be a body!'

'Oh but you must not wish for such things, Sir Laurence. You open Pandora's Box by saying such things.'

'Nonsense old boy, never been superstitious in my life. I survived the war, so nothing that lot can throw at me could affect me in the slightest, and believe me they do. Shall we say eight? Friday? I won't take no for an answer, trust me.'

'I do trust you,' he paused for a moment to reflect on the conversation. Sir Laurence's smile got wider as he waited for the inevitable answer.

'I accept your gracious invitation, Sir Laurence.'

'Invitation? Command, old boy!'

The boat was arriving at the dock when Sir Laurence handed Straay a card with the address. He made a note on the back of the name of the railway station the Dutchman should go to, at what time he should arrive and so on. He was meticulous, Straay noted, repeating the instructions twice to ensure everything was in order. Finally, he shook Straay's hand and with a slight lift of his hat, disappeared off down the deck.

* * * * *

Doctor Pieter Straay narrowed his eyes as he watched Sir Laurence fade into the crowd. An odd sense of foreboding crept through him; one he was unable to shake. Something in the conversation had left a nagging feeling yet, as hard as he tried, he could not determine why. Yes, the invitation was unexpected, but Sir Laurence Gregson had sought him out personally with, clearly, intimate knowledge of who and what he was. This could mean only one thing. Gregson had definitely orchestrated the meeting. The preamble conversation was the hook and the invitation was the goal.

'What could he possibly want with me at the house he couldn't tell me directly on the boat?' Straay asked himself quietly.

The sound of the Steward's voice interrupted his reverie, and he thoughtfully made his way towards the disembarkation point.

About the Author

Christopher D. Abbott is a Reader's Favorite award winning author and a writer of crime, fantasy, science-fiction, and horror. He has a background in human behavioural studies and psychology and loves quirky characters such as Rodney David Wingfield's Inspector "Jack" Frost, Agatha Christie's Poirot, and Sir Arthur Conan Doyle's Sherlock Holmes.

Described by **New York Times** Bestseller Michael Jan Friedman as "an up-and-coming fantasy voice", and compared to Roger Zelazny's best work, Abbott's Osirian series brings a bold re-telling of Ancient Egyptian mythology and presents a fresh view of deities we know, such as Horus, Osiris, and Anubis. He weaves the godlike magic through musical poetry, giving these wonderfully tragic and deeply flawed "gods" a different perspective while increasing their mysteriousness.

Abbott is a keen musician and has written a number of songs—he also likes to get out and play as often as he can. He also volunteers his time to support Chase Masterson's Pop Culture Hero Coalition, a non-profit organisation that champions overcoming bullying and social injustice. He lives in CT. You can contact him at:

Info@cdanabbott.com

cdanabbott@gmail.com

and find him online at:

www.facebook.com/cdanabbott

www.twitter.com/cdanabbott

https://www.instagram.com/cdanabbott/

and at his website:

www.cdanabbott.com

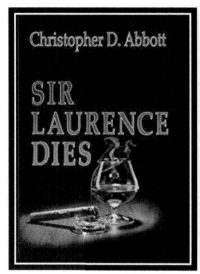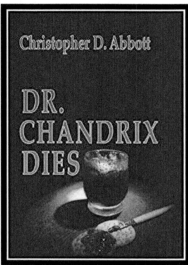

Ancient Egyptian Fantasy

"In his Songs of the Osirian series, Christopher D. Abbott has reinterpreted Egyptian mythology, creating a moving chessboard of gods, demigods, monsters, and men that is by turns alien and familiar--but always exciting. Abbott's armies assail mighty fortresses. His heroes brave benighted landscapes. His lovers endure terrible hardships. And all the while, the shadow of the reborn Beast grows longer and longer, threatening to engulf all of creation.

If you like epic tales of love and hate, loyalty and betrayal, vengeance and forgiveness...if you like chronicles of Good versus Evil, with the highest prize hanging in the balance...you owe it to yourself to read Songs of the Osirian."

Michael Jan Friedman
New York Times Bestselling Author

Available on Amazon & Barns & Noble

Sci-Fi - Horror

More To Fear Than Fear Itself

When a horde of towering creatures wreaks havoc on FDR's Washington D.C., no one–including the president–knows where they came from. A desperate group of survivors makes it to Fort Detrick, where they seek refuge from the devastation. They think they're safe there. After all, It's FDR's state-of-the-art maximum-security facility. But relief turns to horror, as they find they've locked themselves in with a more hideous threat than the one they left behind.

crazy8press.com

The Watson Chronicles

Lieutenant Wilson is found dead at Reardon House, Dartford Kent.

But was it a suicide or a murder?

When Inspector Hargreaves of the Kent Constabulary seeks Sherlock Holmes' aid in uncovering the truth, Holmes and Watson become embroiled in an investigation leading to the heart of Westminster. Possibly to the Crown Herself. Who is Sir Henry Wilburton? What is his connection to the late Professor Moriarty? Holmes must weave a dangerous path if he is to reach a successful conclusion. But with war a possible outcome of failure, the stakes are as high as they can get.

Available on Amazon & Barns & Noble

Printed in Great Britain
by Amazon

12837255R00098